D1394909

Winter's Crimes 19

WINTER'S CRIMES

CRIMES

·19·

edited by
HILARY HALE

MACMILLAN
LONDON

First published in 1987 by
MACMILLAN LONDON LTD
4 Little Essex Street London WC2R 3LF
and Basingstoke

Associated companies in Auckland, Delhi, Dublin, Gaborone, Hamburg, Harare, Hong Kong, Johannesburg, Kuala Lumpur, Lagos, Manzini, Melbourne, Mexico City, Nairobi, New York, Singapore and Tokyo.

British Library Cataloguing in Publication Data

Winter's crimes 19
  1. Detective and mystery stories, English
  823'.0872 [FS]   PR1309.D4

  ISBN 0-333-44516-3

Typeset by Columns of Reading
Printed and bound in Great Britain by
Anchor Brendon Ltd., Tiptree, Essex

Contents

Editor's Note

The tradition of the *Winter's Crimes* series to publish short stories specifically written for each volume continues with this, the nineteenth collection.

The individual talents of the contributors are the best recommendation for the quality of the anthology, and the ten writers have provided a wealth of criminal and murderous entertainment. My thanks go to all the authors for their skills as storytellers and for giving me so much pleasure in bringing them together.

Hilary Hale

Drown Her on Saturday

Celia Fremlin

I wonder how many murderers, potential murderers and would-be murderers there will turn out to be among my readers? More, I suspect, than anyone would guess. But out of all these I wonder if any will have had, or even conceived of, such an experience as mine? The experience, that is, of watching his victim writing out in her own handwriting a clear and accurate account of her own murder; how and when it took place, and where exactly the corpse was to be found. With her own hand, you see, providing proof positive that she must – absolutely *must* – have still been alive after she was dead, if you get my meaning.

You don't? Well, I'd better begin at the beginning, even though the beginning is, I fear, distinctly corny. So much so that you might easily suppose that this is just one more of those Honeymoon Murder stories where the handsome, cold-blooded villain lures the adoring, rich and elderly spinster into marriage, and then scoops the pool.

The pool, in our case, was considerable – the best part of half a million – and though Daphne was not exactly

9

elderly – forty-nine, to be exact, on the very day of her death – she was pretty bloody elderly from my point of view. I am only twenty-eight, you see, and perhaps that was why I was in a bit of a hurry about the whole thing. My youth is precious to me, and naturally I didn't want to waste too much of it on an old bag like Daphne if it could possibly be avoided. A couple of months, I thought, or at most three. And, as it happened, three months was exactly what it was, from the first moment of chatting her up at a Sunday afternoon tea-party, lace doyleys and all, to those final moments of feeling her body go limp under my clenched hands, and checking that her heart had really ceased to beat.

Three months. June, July and August. June for courting her – flowers, love-letters, the whole bloody bit. July for checking out the bank account and making sure that she'd signed all the right papers – she was an absolute child about that sort of thing, Daphne was. Then August, of course, for the wedding, having convinced her at last that it was OK to leave her old cow of a mother to have her strokes and heart-attacks and things on her own. After all, it only takes one to have a stroke or a heart-attack, it's not like sex, or fighting, which of course takes two. And anyway, they were loaded, weren't they? They could afford, couldn't they, to lay on night nurses, day nurses, companions and what-have-you for the old harridan?

Of course, to Daphne, I put all this in a very caring sort of way. 'The best that money can buy,' I said. 'Expert professional attention,' I said. 'She'll be gaining a son,' I said, 'not losing a daughter.' Though of course she *would* be losing a daughter, that was inevitable in the circumstances, but naturally Daphne didn't know this yet. Didn't even suspect it: as I've told you, she was like a child about some things.

In fact, she was like a child about almost everything. Having spent most of her adult life within four walls with an aging invalid, almost everything was new to her, everything was exciting. Our honeymoon cottage with roses round the door (I'd checked this out before making the booking) filled her with idiot rapture. 'Ooh!' she kept saying, and 'Aah!' as we toured the place on that first day. It was really quite peculiar to hear the joyous squeals of a six-year-old emanating from those dry, elderly lips; to watch the radiance of first love illumine that blotchy, wrinkled skin; to feel the trembling of ecstasy in her skinny body. I half expected to hear her bones rattling as she neared her climax.

Because, yes, I did my marital duty by her. I believe this is usual in this sort of set-up? Not that others in the same line of business talk about it much, but it seems like common sense, doesn't it, to allay suspicion? And, anyway, it was only for a month, at most, though of course she didn't know that. 'For ever and ever . . .!' she would babble: 'always . . . always . . .!' and, sometimes, 'What have I done to deserve such happiness?'

Actually, I could have told her what she'd done: she had allowed her senile old mother to make over *everything* to her in order (so I advised them) to avoid death-duties. Would you credit it? Oh, well there's one born every minute: which being so, it's likely that somebody will see to it that one also dies.

Well, anyway, I kept her happy in her fools' paradise for the best part of three weeks, as planned, and then, on Saturday, August 23rd, her forty-ninth birthday, I strangled her. Out in Hambledown Woods, about four miles from here. I'd taken her there for a special birthday picnic, which I'd prepared myself, for a surprise. A pretty commonplace picnic menu, you might say, but, like

I've told you, nothing was commonplace to Daphne. 'Ooh!' she said when she saw the cold roast chicken; and 'Aah!' when she saw the chilled white wine. It's that sort of thing that makes murder easy. In fact, now I come to think of it, 'Ooh!' was the very last thing she said, when she felt my hands sliding up towards her neck . . .

When I say that 'Ooh!' was her very last word, I mean, of course, her very last *spoken* word. Her *written* words were another matter, and I must now explain how it was that her potty old mother (as well as all those nurses and people who would have to read them out to her) continued to get letters from the dead woman for exactly a week after her demise.

It was Daphne's quaint feelings of guilt that made it all so easy – guilt about having gone off to enjoy her honeymoon, leaving the senile old wreck behind her. You would have thought, wouldn't you, that if anyone was suffering pangs of guilt at this point in time it ought to have been me, plotting murder like I was? But no; it had to be Daphne.

'Poor Mumsie, the least I can do is to write her a nice, long, chatty letter *every* day,' she resolved. 'A sort of daily diary of all the funny little happenings, and scraps of news.' Since it was just these funny little happenings and scraps of news that were going to be so important to me, I naturally encouraged the project. Not that it needed any encouragement. She loved me to read her letters as she went along, and I was able to note that, in her childish way, she hardly ever bothered to date them properly. 'Monday, after tea,' she would put; or 'Tuesday, under the big walnut-tree' – that sort of thing. On top of which, she never demurred when I offered to post them for her, so that after she was dead I had a nice selection stored away from which I could choose the appropriate one for sending off with the appropriate postmark.

The first one, the one I posted the very day after strangling her, is the one I remember best:

'Dear Mumsie,

'Don (that's me, by the way) came back from the village with a very sad piece of news this morning. Some poor woman has been found strangled in the woods, only about four miles away. They think she must have been with a friend, as they found the remains of a picnic – cold chicken and white wine . . .'

And so on and so on, exactly as it was subsequently to be. I'd purposely told her this cock-and-bull story in as much detail as I could, and I'd also managed to convince her that poor Mumsie, leading such a dull life as she did, would be enlivened rather than upset by such an exciting story, tragic though it might be.

Watching Daphne writing it all down, word for word the way it was going to happen to her, gave me quite a buzz, I can tell you. It was the best bit of my marriage, really, looking back.

Well, anyway, a week later, as soon as I'd made sure that the body had been discovered, off the letter went. Postmarked *after* the event, you understand, and in her own handwriting describing the murder with perfect accuracy. Enough to get the official knickers in a twist good and proper, wouldn't you say?

Looking back, I feel sure that this one letter on its own would have been enough to clear me completely; but somehow the thrill of bamboozling them all had got into my blood, and I couldn't leave well alone, and so I couldn't resist the prospect of filling out the whole week with more and more incontrovertible evidence that she *must* be still alive.

> '*Monday*. Today we drove to the beach, and Don caught a most *enormous* crab! I was terrified . . .!'

True enough; we had; and I did; and she was. At the time, there was no one around noticing this small happening; but when it came to the replay on the Monday after she was dead, I made sure that half the village noticed. Never mind that the creature, this time, had come from the fishmonger's in a not-too-nearby town – I brandished it in the village pub that evening, making enough song-and-dance about it that they'd all remember. 'My wife won't come in with me – she's terrified!' I laughed, and they all laughed, too, and I wouldn't be in the least surprised if half of them will by now recall actually having *seen* her cowering outside in the car, so good a story did I make of it, to fix it in their minds.

And so on and so on, throughout the post-murder week. Everything that she'd mentioned in her letters as having happened on a given day, I made the carbon-copy of it happen *this* week, on the same day, and making sure that, this time, at least somebody noticed it happening.

Mostly, it was easy, such trivial things did she go on about, any fool could have duplicated them. The only slightly tricky day was Friday, and I wish to God, now, that I'd left it alone. Goodness knows I'd already piled up more than enough evidence, Friday was neither here nor there. But the thing was, Friday was to be the last day of the mirror-image week, and I don't like leaving a job unfinished, not this kind of a job. On the Saturday I was going to get rid of her; a bathing fatality, I thought, at the crowded Bank Holiday beach. 'My wife! . . . I can't seem to see her anywhere . . .! Yes, in a blue bathing-cap . . .

14

She came in ahead of me . . .!' – until the amused chaffing turned into a serious search and into the calling out of life-guards and such and finally into waiting for the body to be washed up at the turn of the tide.

Which of course it wouldn't be. But so what? They aren't, always. A bit of a mystery maybe, but not one to incriminate *me*. How could anyone be supposed to have successfully drowned a hefty, tallish wife under the very eyes of dozens of bathers crowding the sea in every direction? It would be Bank Holiday, remember, and you know what the beaches are like on Bank Holidays, especially during a heat-wave like we happened to be having.

So, as I say, Friday was the last day of which I'd planned a facsimile; and, as I've indicated, it presented slightly more of a challenge than the previous days. But only slightly. It never occurred to me that anything could go seriously wrong:

'*Friday*, after supper:

'Dearest Mumsie,
      '. . . We had quite a little adventure today, driving home from the beach. Taking the bend in the lane rather fast, we landed up on the verge, all among the willow-herb and the scabious and the long grass . . . it was quite a job getting back on the road again, Don had to get out and push . . .'

On that occasion, it happened that no one came by; but this time, of course, someone *was* going to come by; I'd damn well wait there on the verge until they did. 'My wife's gone on ahead to find a phone-box,' I was going to say, to explain how it was that I, a newly-married man, was on my lonesome in this mini-predicament.

15

Exactly how I miscalculated, I'll never know. Two broken legs and a spot of concussion don't leave one's memory in exactly mint condition for details. All I know is, it wasn't a verge, it was some kind of a bloody great ditch, and now here I am in hospital, both legs yanked up to the ceiling, and trying to pretend I'm still unconscious.

'Where's your wife?' they're going to start saying, as soon as they think I can answer. 'What's happened to your wife?'

And I can't think what I'm going to say. The only thing my poor bruised and battered brain seems able to come up with is, 'I've got to drown her! You've got to let me out of here in time to drown her on Saturday . . .! Drown her on Saturday . . . drown her on Saturday . . .'

Nothing in the Library

Winston Graham

I

This was told to me on a winter's night in Cornwall, with the wind crying and rain prattling at the windows. Two-thirds of the story I know to be true. The remaining one-third I cannot vouch for.

II

Mrs Dick Trebarrow died in the autumn of the year. Her husband, the village schoolmaster, had predeceased her by rather less than twenty months. Perhaps village is too undignified a name for Carvossa Road, which is one of those small semi-towns of Cornwall, like Bodmin Road and Grampound Road, which grew up with the advent of a station, built there because a more prosperous and shortsighted neighbour rejected the railways when they were extending over the South-West in the sixties and seventies of last century.

Dick Trebarrow – or Dickie-Boo, as he was called by his pupils – had been a stout, bald, deaf man with three rolls of fat on the back of his neck and an almost satyr-like quality of expression and vitality. Cornish to the backbone, for twenty years until the day he had to retire because of his deafness, he had ruled the school with a rod, not so much of iron as of eloquence. He had a powerful voice, a powerful personality, a powerful hand when he chose to use it. He would have made a wonderful auctioneer. He made a wonderful teacher, except that he was too eccentric and unorthodox and bluntly Cornish to receive preferment. He would hold his fifth and sixth form classes in thrall when he spoke on history, geography or some esoteric subject of his own choice. He could make his pupils see the millions of gallons of water flowing over Niagara just as clearly as the tainted blood of aristocrats flowing from the guillotines of the French Revolution. One of his favourite side-subjects was ghosts and black magic and werewolves, and some of his boys left school better informed on these matters than on quadratic equations.

Mrs Trebarrow, by no means a nonentity herself, did not like Mr Trebarrow, and at a certain stage in her life took to drink, chiefly, it was thought, to annoy him. At least she sobered up a good deal as a widow, so it was a surprise when she died suddenly less than two years after her husband. The doctor put down cardiac failure on her death certificate; her appearance – one of blackened fright – suggested something of the sort, and he had attended her recently for severe indigestion pains. There were no children, and their niece, who had been an occasional visitor to the house, stood to inherit what little they possessed. Preparations were made for the funeral. The body was laid out, the coffin bought, the mourners summoned for Wednesday morning.

The Coroner, Mr Ewart Tonkin, MBE, TD, was a studious, nervous, conscientious man, and on Monday night he could not sleep: whenever he dropped off it was into a nightmare of being pursued by a black dog, from which he shook himself into wakefulness as one climbing out of a pit of slime. He did not remember ever having such dreams before, and he blamed the pigeon pie his wife had made. His wakefulness gave him time to reconsider the matter of Mrs Trebarrow's death and to ask himself whether he had been a shade lax in passing the death certificate so casually. On the Tuesday he rang Dr Harness and told him that in view of Mrs Trebarrow's known alcoholism – even though it might have been less obvious recently – he felt there should have been an inquest, and on reflection he had decided to order this. The funeral could be postponed forty-eight hours.

It was. Mrs Trebarrow was discreetly opened up; it was found she had suffered from a massive infarction and that death had been instantaneous – and natural. The funeral could go ahead.

Friday morning dawned as damp and discreet as a reluctant mourner. Daylight on the first of November always comes slowly; but along with the daylight came the sexton. He had, of course, done the digging on the Tuesday for the Wednesday funeral, and in so doing had exposed the coffin of Mr Dick Trebarrow, lowered into the grave the year before last. Because of the delay in the burial of Mrs Trebarrow, the earlier coffin had been exposed for a couple of days. Nothing untoward in that.

Except that, when the sexton went to the grave that Friday morning a couple of hours before the funeral, just to make sure everything was shipshape and that the sides hadn't crumbled, his first glance in told him that the coffin of schoolmaster Trebarrow had been tampered with. The sexton did not go down to see, but you could tell from ground level that the lid had been unscrewed, and he thought he observed a knee cap and thigh bone sticking up, for all the world as if Mr Trebarrow had been trying to get out.

The vicar, thus informed, went to see for himself and then rang the police. The police came to look and brought with them a surgeon who descended by ladder to investigate. The grave had been rifled. Odd bones lay here and there, most with part of the flesh still on them. A pathologist was called in.

It was clear that between nightfall on Tuesday and dawn on Friday someone had been down, opened the coffin, and disturbed Mr Trebarrow. Indeed, it took time to put Humpty-Dumpty together again. After a while the pathologist, who was good at jigsaws, pronounced that Dick Trebarrow was all there, except for one part of him, which was his head. Someone had stolen schoolmaster Trebarrow's head. The funeral of Mrs Trebarrow was again postponed.

The inspector and the sergeant and the pathologist met over coffee in the police station later that morning to consider what action should be taken. An offence had clearly been committed, but whether this amounted to a misdemeanour or a felony was open to question. Should it not be as much a breach of the common law to steal a man's head as his watch?

Failing the madman or the drunken reveller out for a lark, some motive must be sought. Mr Trebarrow had by no means been universally popular, and among his many former pupils there might be some who nurtured an old and nasty resentment. The open grave had provided the opportunity. But in that case the skull could only have been taken to break up or to throw away on some rubbish dump, and the chances of discovering the culprit were small. Could there be some other, more bizarre and as yet unguessed, motive?

It was the sergeant, an older man than the others and one who had lived in Carvossa Road all his life, who had the memory.

'Seven or eight years gone,' he said, 'there was the scandal . . . you mind it, sur? Nay, 'twas the year you come up from Penzance. Dick Trebarrow was always one for Cornish customs, Cornish rites, old Cornish traditions, like. Mad about 'em. 'Twas All Hallows Eve: he took his sixth form boys up to the top of Torgullick – where the cairns be – and give them a lecture and a demonstration. Some old custom he'd turned up in some book. But next week things leaked out; one boy told his folk; seems not so much an old Cornish custom as wicked, ungodly things. Black Mass, celebrated on the Old Father Cairn, as 'tis called. They all paraded around in black gowns; Trebarrow read out of a book by the light of a lantern, presided, as they d'say. Relics were brought out. There was a right fuss.'

'Well, where does that get us?'

The sergeant was not to be hurried. 'You know what folk are like around here. Chapel-going. Or if no longer chapel-going, belonging to believe most of the things the chapel d'teach. There was a right fuss. Dick Trebarrow were brought up before the school governors. He swore the practice *was* Cornish, but he said anyhow 'twas but a play on his part, miming the old custom. It went back to the Druids, he said. Little different from the Gorsedd, he said. The boys thought 'twas just a lark, he said; too bad if one of 'em took it the wrong way . . . But some of the other boys was questioned and, though they had no complaints, 'twas generally felt Dick Trebarrow had gone much too far. Whether part play or no, 'twas sacrilegious, folk thought, and there was a move that he be dismissed. But nothing came of it, save a public apology to the parents from Trebarrow; so I believe it was mostly overlooked and forgot, after a while. There was a good turn-out for his funeral, I mind.'

'I've already asked you,' said the inspector with a touch of impatience. 'What bearing has all that on this case?'

'Well, sur, I b'lieve in some black magic practices, they d'make use of a skull.'

A thoughtful silence followed. The sergeant stirred his coffee, which had gone cold. The biscuit had made crumbs on the table and he picked them up delicately with his forefinger, one by one. He was a tidy eater.

The pathologist took out his diary. 'By God,' he said. 'Last night was the thirty-first of October.'

'Just so,' said the sergeant, licking his finger. 'As I was about to say, sur. All Hallows Eve.'

III

Just to cover the possibilities, word was sent out to neighbouring police stations, requesting any information about the movement of tramps, or whether any religious sect or anti-religious sect might be wandering the countryside with crazy ideas. Cornwall is a stamping ground for up-country eccentrics.

No other station had anything to report. A man in St Ives had tried to murder his mother-in-law and was likely to be charged with GBH. A car had got out of control in Redruth and had run into a shop window. Otherwise the county was singularly quiet.

Inspector Carter drove up to have a look around Tor-gullick. It was a desolate spot: a half-dozen great stones of prehistoric days, four standing in giant disarray like drunken Paleoliths, two fallen, the largest of these, a huge hump, being known as Old Father Cairn. Sloping away from them was moorland and heath, and not far distant the glimmering pewter of the sea. It was a quiet, peaceful, undisturbed spot, except that someone had recently had a fire near Old Father Cairn. A blackened circle, and some of the heather had been burned and trodden down. Under a stone he discovered some pieces of cardboard with words written on in red ink. A few had been burned, others charred; he couldn't make head or tail of the words that were left. He wondered if the vicar would know.

On the way to the church he picked up Sergeant Davy, who had been to the school, going through the records of seven years ago. Davy reported that there had been nine boys in the sixth form at that time. One of these, the one who had complained, was now living in Bristol. Of the others, one was dead, and the Sergeant was of the opinion that at least three of the rest had also gone away. It left a probable four – and, of course, not to be ignored, nine sets of parents who might have something to contribute if they were politely asked.

They went to see the vicar, a desiccated but learned old man, who told them that yesterday morning on going into church he had found that the altar candlesticks had been carried down to the font and that the crucifix was upside down. Also, there had been a stain on the altar cloth which he had supposed was red paint.

He frowned down at the pieces of cardboard the inspector gave him and then took them away to his study. After ten minutes he emerged, bearing the pieces as if they carried a rare pestilence.

'I . . . er – was distinctly of the opinion – I formed the opinion . . . and – er – the books I have referred to do bear this out. These words.' He put the pieces on the table and wrinkled his nose at them. 'These words – such of them as I can make out . . . DIES, MIES, IESQUET, BENEDOEFET, DOUVIMA, ENITEMAUS. These are the words, are they not, Inspector?'

'I've not idea, sir. I'm afraid I never took Latin. Always supposing they are Latin. Do they mean anything to you, sir?'

'Well, yes, as a matter of fact they do. Pure doggerel, no doubt. But they have been used in the past – according to the books I have referred to – they have been used in the past at what is called a Black Mass, that is for the purpose of conjuring up the Devil.'

IV

Over lunch they examined the list of nine boys, with ticks against the names of those who were still reputedly in the district, and Sergeant Davy said he might as well begin with Ken Annear, though he was of a mind that Annear worked in Launceston and only came home evenings. The next one was Behenna . . .

The inspector said: 'This is such a small place. Folk know so much of each other's business. Who would we ask who might tell us if Trebarrow had a special crony or a special enemy?'

'I did ask at the school, but the other two was both new, and Mr Prior said he'd hardly spoken to Trebarrow since he took over.'

'I'll ring the bookshop,' said the inspector. 'They might

know if anyone has been buying books about these sort of things, black magic and the like.'

He did so. Nobody had. Then, inspired, he tried the County Library, which had a small branch in Carvossa Road. The librarian said, Yes, a young man called Len Highsmith was always in pestering them, asking questions. He had several times been fined the price of a book for saying he had lost it. They had only recently been trying to get him two more books on demonology.

Inspector Higgins set down the telephone and looked enquiringly at Davy.

'Oh, yes, sur,' said Davy, his thumb pressing the paper. 'He's third on the list. I know all about Len.'

He knew all about Len. A loner. Lived with his widowed mother. Worked during the summer months at a hotel on the coast, every winter on the dole. Didn't seem to have many friends. 'Simple?' asked the inspector. 'No, no,' said the sergeant. 'Just a quiet one. Never been in trouble, except the once.' 'What was that?' 'He was warned, that's all. Never came to nothing. He kept sneaking into the church at night, playing notes on the organ. There was a window broken too.'

'Well, you go and call.'

'Yes, sur. And I'll take Sam.'

The Highsmiths lived in one of those long narrow granite streets put up to accommodate working families in the days before Cornwall's tin and copper mines became derelict. Number Twelve was like all the others: two up, two down, lace curtains behind flat sash windows, a rubber plant in the window, a coloured fanlight over the door. Mrs Highsmith was a thin, frail, complaining woman with grey hair pulled back, and chapped hands held in front of a clean nylon apron. After she had got over her indignation at being confronted by Sergeant

Davy and a constable, she showed them into a front room that smelled of mildew, and shouted upstairs.

Len Highsmith came down. A lumpy young man of twenty-three, with short-cropped fair hair and pale prominent eyes of a washed-out blue. His face was expressionless. His eyes were expressionless. He seemed neither surprised by his visitors nor overawed.

Sergeant Davy explained the purpose of their call. Some time between Tuesday night and Thursday night of this last week a grave, just reopened for the burial of a lady recently deceased, had been rifled by a person or persons unknown and part of a previously interred body, that of her husband, Mr Dick Trebarrow, had been taken away. It so happened that enquiries which were in hand had led them to call here . . .

'Oh, yes,' said Len Highsmith. 'He's upstairs.'

V

Len made a statement freely and without hesitation. He'd always, he said, had this thing about the occult – least-wise ever since that first time at Torgullick, when old Dickie-Boo had put on such a show. There was him and another lad who'd been interested special, and they'd always kept in with Mr Trebarrow even after he retired. Because there was all that row with the parents, they'd kept it quiet, but they'd met, just the three of them, at Old Father Cairn atop of Torgullick every Hallowe'en, and practised the occult. 'Nothing wrong in that, I hope? No law against it, is there?'

'No law at all, lad,' said the sergeant. 'Not so far as we've gone.'

26

Last year, Len went on, with Dickie-Boo being dead, there'd been no ceremony, no nothing, nothing at all. Seemed so flat. He hadn't been happy about it. You get to miss things.

'What sort of things?'

'Well, you just miss it, see? Practising the occult.'

'What about the other feller?'

'What other feller? Oh . . . you mean Jack Lanyon. He was dead too.'

'Out swimming, wasn't it, if I remember?'

'Yes, out swimming.'

'Always thought that strange,' said Davy. 'He was a strong swimmer, knew the coast. You don't have many Cornish lads getting themselves drowned.'

For the first time Len showed a slight uneasiness. 'Must have gone out too far.'

'And forgotten to come back, eh?'

'What's that? What's that you mean?'

'Nothing. I was just thinking aloud.' The sergeant glanced at the constable. 'Just thinking aloud, eh, Sam? Tell me, Len, when you was performing other times at Torgullick. The occult, eh?'

'The occult.'

'Did you ever have a skull then?'

'Oh, yes, always. 'Twas an old one Dickie-Boo had bought somewhere . . . second-hand, as you might say. But when he died Mrs Trebarrow broke it up with a hammer. She didn't hold with none of it. Stupid old bitch.' Len sniffed and breathed noisily through his nose. 'My mum, she don't mind at all. Doesn't have to.'

'Jack Lanyon,' said the sergeant. 'Did it prey on his mind?'

'What?'

'What you was doing.'

27

'Ar . . . Maybe. Mr Trebarrow said he'd no bottle.'

'No bottle?'

'Didn't like to go through with it, see?'

'Through with what?'

'Oh, this and that.'

'Which you did, eh?'

'Yes, I suppose.'

There was an uneasy silence. They could hear the clatter of dishes from the kitchen. Such a wholesome sound.

'This year . . . Did you do it all on your own?'

'Yes, more or less.'

'What do that mean?'

'Means yes. Since Dickie-Boo went . . .'

There was a further pause.

'All on your own, eh?' said Davy.

Len said: 'To understand, you have to be a believer, see?'

'No, I don't. What d'you do up there on the Cairn?'

'Just the occult,' said Len. It was his favourite word. One didn't know what multitude of sins against the Holy Ghost it covered.

Sergeant Davy squared his shoulders. 'Oh, well, we'd best collect the evidence, hadn't we, eh? Is it – you say it's upstairs?'

'Oh, you don't want to worry. I took him Wednesday to the beach, cleaned him out. Got him real clean, rubbed him with small stones. Got all the brains out. Then I polished him with sandpaper. When you use something like that you have to have it *clean*. Even so . . .'

They waited.

'Yes?'

Len swallowed and licked his lips. 'They oughter have got me them books from the library. 'Tis no sort of a library service. It could've gone better.'

'What could?'

'The service. There was a bit of a mix-up. But it all come right in the end.' He sniffed again. 'You don't have to worry. He's all nice and *clean*.'

They found him so.

VI

The head – or skull – of Mr Trebarrow was duly returned to its rightful owner. Len Highsmith was charged with desecration of graves under some ancient statute which had lain on the books about half as long as witches had inhabited Endor. He was fined £10, which, the magistrate said, was the maximum penalty under this statute. Fifty-five books on black magic were found in Len's bedroom, and he was fined £20 for having borrowed some of them from other libraries and not returned them.

No mention in court was made of various other items found in the bedroom, such as a goose's foot, a hare's ears, a raven's head (smelling somewhat), a selection of dogs' and cats' teeth, and what was eventually recognised as a much-withered viper with most of the head missing.

Giving evidence on behalf of her son in court, Mrs Highsmith was loud in complaint against the libraries about the whole affair. At first it was thought she was complaining because the libraries had furnished her son with too many books; but it later became clear that she was saying that they had not done enough. If, she said, the County Library had been up to the job, the other books would have supplied her son with all the information he needed without him having to engage in grave robbery. The logic of this was not plain, and the magistrates listened to it impatiently and then turned to the next case.

There the matter ended – or should have ended – or perhaps did end. Only Sergeant Davy, the oldest and most observant person concerned, was not so sure. He saw Len Highsmith occasionally over the next few months, and as the months grew into years. The young man kept very much to himself, and was generally shunned by his fellows. He was known to have got hold of another skull, legitimately this time, but no one ever saw him up at Torgullick, and if he practised his forbidden rites it was in place or places unknown. He put on weight rapidly, taking no exercise, and as he grew fatter he lost his hair. Three rolls of fat began to develop on the back of his neck. He was also going deaf.

A visiting journalist, soon after the Trebarrow affair, tried hard to persuade Len to tell him exactly what took place at the ceremonies at Torgullick. Len was not forthcoming, but after the fourth pint he did open up a little. He leaned a shirt-sleeved elbow on the bar and said:

'Well, see, 'tis like this. 'Tis all to do with the carrying away of condemned souls, see? They're bound to this earth and they need to be released. They're looking for somewhere to hide.'

'Hide? I don't know what you mean exactly.'

'Well . . . another body, or another Church. Mind . . .'

The journalist waited. 'Well?'

'Mind, they look some frightful when they come up out of the fire. They're blacker than pitch, these souls, they've teeth like lions, nails on their fingers like wild boars, and horns on their foreheads with poison dripping. They've got cloven feet and wide ears flowing with corruption, and they discharge wiry worms from their nostrils.'

The journalist tapped his notebook but did not write anything.

'You having me on?'

Len smiled. 'I reckon. Just wondered how much you'd take.'

But Len's smile was not nice. It was more like a sneer, and showed his teeth. Somebody clacked a beer glass down on the counter behind the reporter, and he jumped.

'There's nothing pretty about the occult,' said Len. 'See. 'Tis all to do with corruption and the worm that dieth not.'

The reporter didn't think his readers would want to know about that. 'This Mr Trebarrow. Great friend of yours, was he?'

'Oh, yes.'

'Didn't you think it wrong . . . doing what you did . . . rifling . . . you know?'

Len laughed. His breath had an unpleasant smell. ''Tis what he wanted.'

There was a long pause.

'Ah,' said the reporter. 'I never know when you're joking.'

A Family Decision

Patricia Highsmith

'Not finishing your pie? You love lemon pie!' Beatrice peered through her blue-rimmed glasses at Roger's dessert plate. Her glasses had over-large round rims, the blue did not go with her reddish hair, and Roger had been reminded a couple of times of an insect, maybe a praying mantis.

He attempted a good-natured shrug. He stirred cream into his coffee, and his fingers tried to put the spoon on the saucer, but the spoon fell to the tablecloth. His right hand was the less reliable. 'Had enough. V' guo' pie, though.' Roger was thinking of something else.

They got the waiter and Roger paid, trembling, with his Visa card. Roger had Parkinson's disease, it had been diagnosed a year or so ago, and he'd had it longer. In the last few months, life had become worse and harder for him.

'I'll drive,' said Beatrice at the car. 'You look tired.'

Roger acquiesced by going round to the passenger side of the car. He had driven to the restaurant, knowing he shouldn't be driving, because his muscles were slow, but he drove only in the neighbourhood where the speed limits were low. Roger didn't trust his wife's driving. She was impulsive, always thought the other car in the wrong. But maybe a car accident was as good a way to die as any, for both of them. A good *crash* at speed might kill them instantly, and would that be so bad, after all? But they were going to drive home through a residential area and at not more than thirty miles an hour. Then, too, Roger wouldn't want anyone else to be killed or hurt because of his wife's driving.

He winced as Beatrice went through a STOP sign at normal speed, and Beatrice laughed her short, suppressed-sounding laugh, as if she were genuinely amused. Roger hated the laugh; it came at inappropriate times.

'Hardly any traffic at this hour.' She sat back in a relaxed manner at the wheel, stared straight ahead as if there were no potential danger from right or left, and Roger had the feeling that she too might be thinking of something else now, a feeling he'd had on other occasions when she drove.

But surely she was not thinking of the same thing he was. Beatrice was full of plans, happy things to do in the future: maybe acquiring a larger house in town, one with a swimming pool that she had seen; helping their daughter Dot and her husband do up the summer cottage they had recently bought just a couple of miles out of town; even taking a cruise on the Nile with 'a neighbour' or with Dot, if Dot would take the time away from her child psychiatry work. Roger knew that the helping Dot and Joe idea would come to naught, as would the Nile cruise idea with neighbour or Dot, because neither the neighbours nor Dot could stand Beatrice for more than half an hour at a time. Couldn't Beatrice see that?

Roger's thoughts, on the other hand, were of death and

dying. His days were numbered, as the saying went, and he'd already enjoyed more than he had expected to after his doctor's diagnosis and comments.

They were home, the big comfortable car eased itself into the garage, doors slammed shut, locked.

The house was lovely, two-storeyed, lived-in, a mixture of leather and cosy upholstery in the living room, books, an abstract sculpture of wood some three feet high by a friend of Roger's on a big round table, two of Roger's own paintings on the walls. Sometimes the living room looked quite new, interesting to Roger, and sometimes utterly old hat, insufferably familiar, like the four walls of a prison. Odd what living with a death sentence did to one's outlook.

'I think I'll tackle those lower drawers tonight,' Beatrice said with a peppy air, two minutes after they'd got home. She was already kneeling on the oriental rug, pulling a bottom drawer of the welled desk completely out.

This happened, or something similar, every evening. Beatrice was a night owl. But usually she did not announce her project.

Roger leaned his cane against the back of the chesterfield, awkwardly removed his blue blazer, and went and hung it in the hall closet. He didn't need his cane so much in the house, where there were chair backs and stair rails to hang on to. This evening the old living room did look subtly different, and Roger realised why: this was the last evening he would be gazing at it like this, with the summer evening's faint light still at the window, with a single lamp on near where Beatrice knelt, her ample rump higher than her head. By this time tomorrow, the deed should be done. It had to be. He expected it of himself. He'd need his cane then, it was a major part of his plan – major because Beatrice would notice any other 'weapon' he might be carrying, such as a hammer. Where would they take him afterwards? Roger wondered. To an ordinary prison? Why not? Prisons had hospital wings.

'Roger, remember this? Picture of us in Venice when Dot was about six?' She held up an enlarged photograph.

Roger leaned forward to see. 'Yes – yes, I remember.'

He stared unblinkingly at Beatrice, who had gone back to her rummaging, sorting, throwing away. She was a large woman, quite as tall as he, because his illness seemed to have shrunk him, though of course a slouch now took from his height too. And he had lost weight. He realised how absurd he would look to an observer, tackling Beatrice – something like David attacking Goliath! Yet David had won, with a stone. Roger intended to begin with a push. And he would succeed. Starting at the top of the cellar steps. He would put so much willpower into his push that he couldn't lose! He'd crawl on the cellar floor, if necessary, grasping her ankles, even if she kicked him blind, and he would do what had to be done. His intention was to strangle her, after perhaps a stab with the cane in the throat. Horrible to imagine, and certainly more easily imagined than done, he realised. After she had fallen down the cellar steps, he would follow, hoping that she'd be knocked out, or at least half knocked out, so that he could do the rest with the aid of the cane, which he'd still have in hand. He had thought of having a hammer within reach down there, hadn't arranged that yet, and now it might be too late for the hammer, as Beatrice would think it odd if he went down to the cellar tonight – she might notice if he did – and he was determined to do it tomorrow.

Determined. He stared at Beatrice, tried to grasp his underlip between his teeth, and failed. He could, of course, change his mind. He had thought of this at least

36

three times that day. But something kept him going in the direction he had chosen, or decided on. *Do it.* Do a service before you die. What've you got to lose, Roger Brook? And he had a lot to gain. He could bequeath something to his daughter: freedom from her mother, freedom from years of haggling of a kind that might never reach a conclusion. With Beatrice gone, Dot and her husband Joe and their two children, a boy and a girl ten and twelve now, would inherit all of Roger's paintings, drawings and so on, and the house here which was worth nearly a million, and which Dot and Joe both loved and would enjoy. And then there was the apartment in New York.

'Frozen like a statue?' asked Beatrice, getting to her feet.

'I . . . No . . . Jus . . .'

'Did you have a bowel movement today? You didn't, did you?'

Roger's thoughts shut off, even the scene before him vanished, as if a dark curtain had fallen. He closed his eyes, so hating Beatrice's question and her insect-like gaze turned on him that he was not even trying to put together an answer. True, constipation was one of the annoying accompaniments of Parkinson's. His condition required hot lemon juice (not always efficacious), laxatives often, sometimes an enema. Roger considered it *his* problem, his and his doctor's, like his occasional nausea and cramp.

'. . . *enema*, if you'd like,' Beatrice said, gazing at him, hanging on to the subject.

Roger shook, partly from nervous anger. Sometimes she'd bring it up at a dinner table of six or eight people. '*My* problem – ne'er mind – *please.*'

He turned and headed down the long hall towards his

studio, right foot scraping on the Spanish tile floor. Fumbling, in the dark, he found the light switch left of the door inside, pushed it on, and at once began to relax. The room was long, its width in pleasant proportion. A glass roof slanted down and ended at the top of wooden racks full of canvases. A dozen of Roger's paintings were at once visible, a few leaned against walls, others were propped up on long paint-spattered tables, a couple were hung. At least three were nudes of Beatrice, hardly recognisable not only because she had been younger and more slender when the paintings were done, but because Roger's work was not all that realistic. The reddish hair had hardly changed. Roger was fond of russet and shades of brown.

His right hand moved towards a tin can full of brushes, as if his right arm had a life of its own, but now his forearm shook; it was only depressing to pick up a brush and see how badly it shook, so Roger did not. Still, he loved the smell of his studio, loved the workworn tables. And this was the last evening he would gaze at his studio, or stand here. Terrible, hardly believable, thought. Dot will take care of the studio, keep it practically just as it is, Roger realised, and the realisation was like a safety net that caught him.

An electric typewriter sat on a table in a corner, with the Giacometti-thin black lamp, which Dot had recently given him, beside it. On the table also was a little stack of unanswered letters. Fan letters, well-wishing letters. So many people all over the world seemed to know that he was ill! Dot had helped him answer a few letters, typing his words, being encouraging when he had had to abandon his right hand for his left, in signing.

'It's still *your* signature, Pop,' she had said the other evening. Then with a smile of contempt that Roger seldom saw, 'Mom's in the living room looking at *stock* portfolios now.'

Dot didn't like her mother, and that dated from a long way back, to when Dot had been eight or nine, and Beatrice had begun going out with her own circle of friends in Paris, leaving Dot in Roger's charge. Roger could remember many evenings when Dot had fallen asleep on the couch in his studio, and Roger had gone on working until very late. In her teens, Dot had shown an interest first in medicine and then psychiatry, and had finally elected to study child psychiatry. It was as if Beatrice had sensed that if Dot studied child psychiatry, Dot would soon learn how selfish, even cruel her mother had been to her. Dot had learned this, Roger was sure, but Dot even at seventeen and eighteen had never had a quarrel, or a real showdown, with her mother. It might've been better if they'd had one. As it was, Beatrice was simply aware that her daughter did not like her.

Roger heard Beatrice's step, her heels, in the hall, and she knocked and opened the door at the same time.

'Rodg? Telephone. It's Dot. Sorry, but you'd never let a phone be put in *here*.'

He had started his walk towards the living-room telephone. 'Z-zank you, Bee . . . trice.' He had heard the remark about his telephoneless studio a hundred times.

'Hello, *Pop!*' said Dot's voice. 'We're in the neighbour-hood, had dinner in town and we'd like to come by. OK? I thought it was Mom's lotto night, but I was mistaken.' She gave a laugh. 'How are you, Pop?'

'Same, thank you, m-my love. Yes . . . c-come on . . . by.' His voice sounded like an old man's, ugly and depressing. Old at sixty-two!

Roger passed Beatrice in the hall.

'It's rather late,' said Beatrice. 'I told Dot not to keep

you up long.' Her greenish-grey eyes were mere slits now.

He tried to shrug, and said nothing. What had she been doing in his studio for the past three or four minutes?

Dot seemed to arrive almost at once. 'Pop!' she called, knocking.

And in she came, smiling, with two packages in her arms, both gift-wrapped as if it were Christmas.

'Just some Jack Daniel's for your studio,' she said. 'This one. And the other . . .' She paused as if she'd forgotten. 'Oh, cashews, walnuts and raisins. My mixture. Good for you.' She pushed her fingers through her shortish straight hair. Her hair was brown, with barely a hint of red, her eyes also brown, like Roger's own. 'How're you really feeling, Pop? *Open* one of these. Or I'll do it for you. And sit down!'

'Where's Joe?'

'He went to see his friend Van Salter. Van's an architect too. Didn't I mention him? Lives near here. Joe'll come in a few minutes.' She found a couple of glasses, smudged rather permanently with the remains of white paint and turpentine, rinsed them at the sink, and made two small drinks of half water, half whisky. She wore tan trousers that fitted closely like jodhpurs and a lightweight jacket that she had unzipped. 'You know, Pop, it's indecent the way she's taken over . . . lately.' Dot said this after her first sip, frowning slightly. 'It's going to be hell,' she went on in a soft voice, rather as if she were talking to herself. 'All this . . .' Her eyes swept the room walls and returned to her father.

Was Dot going to propose something? he wondered. Changing his will? He knew she meant that her mother was going to lay claim to most of his works, certainly what Beatrice thought was 'the best' of his paintings, sketches, sketchbooks. According to Roger's latest will, which was now about ten years old, his estate and art works went half to Dot and half to Beatrice. Individual works weren't mentioned, and they should be, Roger knew, but it was a task he had postponed, even after he had learned that he had a serious disease. His will was in the charge of his lawyer, and his art works were handled by Sylvester Galleries Management of New York and London. But Beatrice had her own New York lawyer now and he had a copy of the will, Roger was sure, and Beatrice had not hinted to Dot or Roger what she was up to. No extra settlement would compensate Beatrice for not having been given the lion's share, ninety per cent or so, Roger supposed. Dot had never asked him to change his will, but she had asked him to label things, bequeath them to her or Beatrice 'to save quarrelling'. Talking with his own lawyer, there seemed to be no quarrel in sight, Roger recalled. Lawyers spoke in terms of money sums. Individual paintings, alas, changed value according to the bidding, and the sentiment of the person trying to acquire the paintings.

'I hate to talk like this,' Dot said, 'as if you were already gone.' She slid off the high stool she had perched herself on, knelt beside him and took his hand, his right hand. 'Poor Pop. You've done your best, I know. You have a marvellous patience. Fantastic.' She stood up. 'But she's got nothing better to do with her time than fight . . . And she adores money.'

I know, I know, Roger thought, and let his head nod as it wanted to do. 'I know, my d-dear.'

Now his daughter gave a smile, and patted his shoulder. 'We shouldn't talk like this – as if you're dying tomorrow. You're not dying tomorrow or even next year! Who's to say you *are*?'

In the seconds as his daughter spoke, Roger felt a vague guilt for having married Beatrice Mallett, his model for three years by the time they married, and then pregnant with Dot. Roger had not married Beatrice merely because she was pregnant; he had loved her, he remembered well. He had been aware that she had a simpler background than he, that she hadn't had much schooling, but at twenty-two and twenty-five, as she and he were respectively, Roger had been convinced that such things didn't matter. Well, of course they *didn't*, but unfortunately Beatrice had a selfish and acquisitive side. And money had gone to her head, once Roger had started selling well. In fact, she had done her best to be a snob. Roger had had to see some of his old friends on the sly, some wouldn't come to his and Beatrice's apartments in Europe or to this Connecticut house now, and none of them liked the atmosphere that Beatrice created or exuded.

Roger tried to shift his feet, rolled to one side in his chair.

'Get you something, Pop? Have another drop?'

'N-no, thanks. J-just tired of sitting in one p'sition.' He heard a car door slam.

'There's Joe! I'll bring him in for a minute; all right, Pop? He'll want to say hello.' She dashed off.

Roger spent the next seconds getting to his feet, making sure his shirt was tucked properly into his trousers, squaring his shoulders so he wouldn't look like a hunchback. Then the tall figure of Joe was before him, Joe grinning, extending a hand.

'How are you, sir? Good to see you!'

Was it? Roger put on the best cheer he could. 'Welcome . . . Joe!'

Joe wandered about, looking at the paintings and

sketches like someone at an art show. 'I do enjoy coming in here, Roger.' He looked from Roger to Dot. 'I think your dad's looking pretty good tonight, don't you, Dot?'

'Yes!' Dot went on, saying something else, pleasant nonsense.

Roger did not believe them, but the words were nice to hear. He tried to level out his crooked mouth to a socially acceptable line, and blinked to get rid of the doltlike stare that he saw on his face sometimes when he glanced at a mirror, or when he shaved, for instance. But the younger people were not looking at him. They were a few yards away, Joe pointing at a lithograph in sepia colour of a nude child seated in a straight chair: Dot, aged about eight.

'Y-you f-fanshy . . . zat?' asked Roger, raising his brows, questioning. He pulled a handkerchief from a pocket quickly, to catch saliva that dropped from a corner of his mouth. 'Take . . . *take* it, Joe.' Roger gestured with his left hand, insisting.

'Pop means it! It'll please him!' Dot said, and when Joe hesitated, she lifted the glass-fronted litho from its hook on the wall. 'Now, Joe, out the side door and into the car.' She thrust the picture towards him. 'No argument. See you in two minutes.'

Joe went. 'Thank you, sir. G'night,' he said before he vanished out of the white door at the back of the studio.

'Pop . . .' Dot's brown eyes looked straight into his. 'I wasn't on the track of your changing your will even to make things more definite – who gets what. I don't think that would do enough good to make it worth the trouble. She'd still argue. The four or five pictures Joe and I have of yours . . . we'll never sell. We love them too much. It's just that I'd have liked a couple of sketchbooks, for instance – something personal. I suppose you can call me

43

greedy.' She moved, ready to leave.

Roger moved too, towards a long table at the back of which stood a row of some thirty sketchbooks and tablets, many spiral-backed, of varying sizes. 'Can't . . . reach 'em.' He gestured, slid his left forearm ineffectively on to the table. 'Take . . . take a couple. She's – sh . . .'

'Thank you, dear Pop! *I'll* be quiet, don't worry.' Dot leaned across the table and took two tablets out carefully, as if they might fall apart, but they were not particularly old. These were watercolour and pen and ink sketches.

Roger had wanted to say, 'She won't miss 'em,' but he had not been quick enough. The studio was empty again, save for the echo of Dot's 'Bye-bye' and her promise to telephone him tomorrow. Roger sat down on an old wooden straight chair and poured (using both hands) half an inch of Jack Daniel's into his glass which still held a bit of the drink Dot had made. Tomorrow he was going to eliminate Beatrice, he reminded himself, as he might of a chore he must not forget or shirk.

He reminded himself also that he had reasoned his way to this decision, and that there should be no going back now. Nevertheless, he was realist enough or human enough to think about the reality of the deed, not merely of the height and strength of Beatrice, but of the fact that she was a human being like himself, like any woman who might be a friend or a neighbour. He intended to end a human life. Was it better to let that fact sink in or to avoid it, if he wanted to gain fortitude for tomorrow? Roger decided that it was better to confront the fact. He fancied (realising that perhaps he flattered himself) that he had always been such a person, willing and able to face facts and weigh them before making a move.

Consequently, he tried to foresee what he would do tomorrow. And at what time? The cleaning woman Vera was not due tomorrow. Maybe a delivery from the wines and spirits shop was, but they hadn't a key to the house. Anyway, how long would it take? A warmness of terror spread over Roger suddenly, his feet moved on the floor. *Minutes*, it would take. That was reality, something one saw on the face of a watch. Five minutes, more, after he pushed her down the stairs?

Roger found his throat dry, lifted his wobbling glass and drank, and stared into space.

Maybe only four minutes, he thought, but they had to be of concentrated effort. He would be hoping that Beatrice was knocked unconscious by the fall, but he supposed that there was about one chance in four that this would happen. He'd go down the stairs as quickly as he could (the stairs had a rail), and make use of the cane. The reality of striking her, of driving the end of his cane into the soft throat shocked him. But it was either the cane or his fingers and thumbs, and his hands hadn't the strength, he knew. If Beatrice lifted one of her powerful knees . . . And, too, she might scream. That was likely. But that wouldn't matter, if he could get it done before anyone came. Nearest neighbours were a hundred and fifty yards distant and might not be in, he reflected. No, no one was going to hear her unless it be the unlikely delivery boy or man. Roger finished his glass.

He'd been over all this before, the human aspects of it, or the inhuman. Was he going to paralyse himself like Hamlet, going over and over it and doing nothing finally?

Roger stood up, and held to the chair's back. There crossed his mind a memory of happy days with Beatrice in Villefranche, a time of sunlight and open windows. And the especially happy times in Majorca, where Dot had been conceived. They had been happy times for Beatrice too, he was sure. Later, she had had a few brief affairs on the side. And so had he, he allowed. On that score, they were perhaps even. He couldn't recall who had been unfaithful first, was inclined to think that Beatrice had, then thought he might be trying to bolster his side of things by thinking that. His *side*? Wrong word. There were no 'sides'. Ten years ago Roger had suggested to Beatrice that they might divorce. *Shouldn't* they? he had asked. Dot had been in her twenties, there had been no other person in the picture then, for him or Beatrice, but they weren't happy together any longer, seemed insufferably ill-suited (had they ever been well suited?), and Roger had offered to settle a nice income on Beatrice, to give her this house plus the New York apartment, if she wanted them. He recalled the blank and somewhat frightened look on Beatrice's face when he had mentioned divorce. Almost trembling, at least in her voice, she had said no, she didn't want a divorce, and how absurd of him to think of divorce!

Wasn't it a marriage like a few million others? Roger asked himself. Many aging men and women were mildly or maybe very unhappy with their spouses, but how many in their mid-sixties thought it worth it to divorce? Or to make any changes?

Roger pushed the straight chair, aligned it with the table's edge, and turned towards the door.

What would the world think of him? Some independent part of Roger didn't give a damn. Another part did care, because of Dot and his two grandchildren, Roger and Daniela. *Murderer*. Would they call him that? Would that outweigh the relief he had brought them by ridding them of Beatrice? Weren't his paintings more important than his behaviour in his private life? Were people suddenly going to say that his work wasn't good, or that its artistic value had slumped? If he was now commanding around a million for a large painting, was that price going to tumble? Things didn't work that way. Not in the art world.

Roger looked with a frown, critically, at a large painting, wider than it was high, of Paris house tops. The colours were chiefly reddish brown and dark blue, the house tops more abstract than realistic. Roger had been offered a great deal for *View from Rue Monsieur-le-Prince*, he forgot just how much. He had never wanted to part with it. He'd done it in his mid-twenties. Now it would go to Dot. Soon. A nice thought. He switched off the last light, the one by the door, and went out.

The next morning did not go as smoothly as he had hoped. Beatrice had an engagement with Lydia Marsh at a quarter to eleven: Beatrice was to meet Lydia in Forster's, the town department store, and help Lydia decide on wallpaper for a guest room in her house. Beatrice also wanted to paper an upstairs room, she'd mentioned it weeks ago, so it seemed they were going to help each other with wallpaper selection. Beatrice said she would be back by half-past noon at the latest.

'Take your pills this morning, Roger?'

She meant the L-dopa. 'Yes, I . . . I did . . . zanks for . . .' He let it go.

Beatrice went off in the car.

This gave Roger the opportunity to put a hammer in a convenient place. Roger carried the hammer (the one from the kitchen drawer) down the cellar steps, taking his cane at the same time, and he tried descending as rapidly as possible, an activity which left him a bit short of breath, and he'd need breath, he told himself. He laid the hammer on a wooden sideboard which was part of the wine racks and about five feet from the foot of the stairs.

He had a distinct feeling or premonition that he would not use the hammer. Was he losing his nerve for the whole venture?

He looked up at the stairs, which had some fourteen steps, as if they were a mountain he had to climb. His mouth hung open, breathing. The stairs were in a corner against one wall, with a handrail on their outer side. He would have to give her a mighty shove, Roger realised. He envisaged Beatrice grasping the banister at once, saving herself neatly, turning on him with a furious face.

And what a splendid moment or opportunity for her to finish him off, Roger thought: in a moment of wrath, which Beatrice would surely have, on the right scene, the cellar steps and the cement floor below. She wanted him dead as soon as nature would oblige, of that Roger was sure. She could afford to remind him to take his various pills, because the pills weren't going to save him. But once he'd given her the idea of the cellar steps – why, that would be so much quicker, and she could say he'd fallen!

Roger imagined Beatrice with the same problem: he lying dazed on this cement floor, but still alive, she with the task of killing him, maybe reaching for the hammer. He shut his eyes, then looked at his watch, saw that it was well past eleven, and started up the stairs.

He found, by checking his watch, that it took him nearly two minutes to get up the stairs.

And now the telephone was ringing. Splendid, Roger thought, if Beatrice had had a fatal accident by cruising through a STOP. But he knew it would not be. 'Hello?' he said at the living-room telephone.

'Hello, *Roger*! Hubert here.' Hubert Barrow's voice was cheerful. 'I wish to report a sale. *Studio with Rainbow*. Remember we agreed to ask a few thousand more than the catalogue price?'

Roger only vaguely remembered, but said he did remember. Hubert had got the price. The news did not cheer Roger. He remembered the painting distinctly, was fond of it but not in love with it. The buyer, Hubert said, was a Mrs Kershaw of Dallas, acting for . . . Hubert said the name, but Roger was not listening. Hubert, in New York, would write all this in a letter which would arrive tomorrow or the next day, and possibly be opened by Dot, a few days from now. Roger had no secretary.

'That's nice news,' Roger said.

''Tis a nice pot o' money. And how're you doing?'

Just a few months ago, Hubert had asked, 'What're you working on now, Rodg?' Roger replied the usual, that he was managing pretty well, thanks.

When he hung up, Roger returned to the matter at hand. Would he tell Beatrice of a wine delivery in her absence, one they hadn't been expecting, had they? And would she take a look to see if it was their usual? Or would she go at once to the telephone to bawl out Carlson's Wines and Spirits?

Roger was in the kitchen, watering the plants on the sills – one of his daily chores considered therapeutic – when he heard the car. Beatrice was back. Where had the time gone?

Beatrice came bustling in through the door from the garage into the kitchen, her arms full of plastic bags out of which rolls of paper protruded. 'Went by the post office to mail something and they gave me this. Whew!' She dropped the bags on a table, and handed Roger the Express letter which had been between her fingers. 'Quite a successful morning! Lydia was pleased.'

'Oh? Good,' said Roger, and he opened the envelope because he had nothing else to do just then, Beatrice being occupied with dragging rolls of paper out, folding the plastic shopping bags to go into the bag reserve.

The letter was from a New York TV programme manager, respectfully asking permission to visit him with a view to discussing a one-hour or a ninety-minute documentary on his life and work.

> '. . . Your fee would of course be in the five-figure range . . . We would appreciate a reply at your earliest convenience, as such a project requires . . .'

Now or never, Roger thought, jolted back to Beatrice. This was not the first such letter he had received. The world could not wait to write his obit. Now or never, he thought, and said, 'By the way . . . Carlson's delivered a case of some-zing. Did we order wine?'

'I didn't . . . This morning?' Beatrice looked surprised.

'Y-yes. Want to take a look? M-maybe we can use it.'

She went at once to the cellar door, because Carlson's always carried down the cases. Beatrice wore yellow shoes with medium heels, a full black skirt with many rows of black lace, a white blouse. As she took the second step down, she having put on the light, Roger gave her a hard push in the small of the back.

Beatrice fell forward with a little shriek of surprise, as if she hadn't breath at that instant for a scream, failed to grasp the banister with her left hand, and then hit the cement floor with a mingled plop and crack sound. And was motionless.

Roger followed, with his cane. Frowning, gasping, one step at a time, Roger descended. Beatrice had still not moved. Roger set his teeth. This was the awful part, but there was the merciful hammer in view, within reach. Roger reached for it, but his shaking right hand stopped midway. With his left hand, he got a handkerchief from a back pocket, and wiped his lips. No, he couldn't, he simply *couldn't* touch her again. The back of Beatrice's neck was exposed, as her longish russet hair had fallen to one side. He was supposed to press the tip of his cane into her throat at the front, to crush the bones there.

'B-bee-*trish*!' Roger called involuntarily, with cracking voice. Now he saw an area of blood forming under her head, where her brow and forehead touched the cement floor.

Maybe she wasn't dead, Roger thought, and would come to and accuse him. So be it. One thing he was sure of, he could not touch her. He turned shakily towards the stairs, got finally up them and stood, recovering his wind, and as soon as he was able went to the telephone in the living room. The number of the town hospital was prominently displayed inside the front cover of the directory, along with the numbers of the police and fire departments.

When the ambulance came, and a couple of young men and a doctor entered the house and went down the cellar stairs, Roger was prepared to say, 'I pushed her.' Beatrice was dead. Roger heard the word 'dead'. So little time had passed, Roger had thought she might be merely unconscious, even though she had bled (a very little bit, he saw now, looking down the cellar steps), and that the interns could revive her, take her to the hospital for shock. Roger did say, 'I pushed her down,' but no doubt it did not come out clearly, and the men were not interested.

'Concussion . . . fracture . . .' The doctor took some notes, standing in the hall, writing in his tablet. He asked the time it had happened, and Roger said about five minutes to noon.

'Would you like a sedative, Mr Brook? . . . Is there

someone who can come and stay with you today?'

'I'll call my d-dutt-r.'

The rather young doctor said he would wait until his daughter arrived, and he urged Roger to sit down. The doctor dialled Dot's number for Roger. No need to announce to the doctor, Roger knew, that he had Parkinson's disease, and that under the best of circumstances he had a devil of a time dialling.

Dot was in. The doctor passed the telephone to Roger.

'H'lo, D-dot. 'S been some . . . an accident here . . .'

'You *fell*, Pop? . . . Pop?'

Roger shook. He gladly let the doctor take the telephone.

'This is Doctor Vance of Barton Memorial. Your mother had a fall down the stairs. Cellar stairs . . . Yes, I'm afraid so. She had a bad fracture and it was fatal.'

Dr Vance insisted that Roger lie back on the sofa, and gave him a glass half full of water with some kind of powder in it, which he said was a mild sedative, and asked if he could bring any of Roger's usual medicine to him. Roger said no, because he had taken his prescribed pills earlier that day.

Dot arrived. Dr Vance again stated that her mother had had a fall down the cellar steps and suffered a head fracture, possibly a broken neck. Her mother's body would be at Barton Memorial until advice came from the family.

When the door had closed on the doctor, Roger concentrated on getting a statement out to Dot. Dot sat on the sofa beside him, pressing his left hand in both hers.

'I . . . I push-ht her . . . down zose shteps,' Roger said.

Dot's brown eyes frowned, and she shook her head. 'Pop, don't *talk* like that. You're upset just now. Sit back . . . relax.'

'But I did . . . I *did* . . . jush as she was starting *down* . . .' He saw doubt, then belief, gather in his daughter's face.

'Is that *true*, Pop?' she whispered.

'Y-y . . .' Roger nodded.

Dot got up from the chesterfield, and went into the hall. Roger supposed she was going to look down the cellar steps, maybe go down. The blood spot, he remembered. Wasn't it still there? Roger heard water running in the kitchen. The truth always came out, did it not? And since he was dying, would be dead in a couple of months, he was sure, what did it matter? He'd confess to the police, die in a prison hospital, and what would it matter?

His daughter returned, and sat beside him again. She had rolled up the sleeves of her pink and white striped shirt, and her hand that gripped his was moist.

'I washed up the blood, Pop. Don't think about it . . . I'm sure no one will mind that I washed it up. I mean . . . the police or such.' She spoke softly, more slowly than usual. 'No one's going to ask questions, Pop, or they'd have been here by now . . . Mom *fell* down those steps. Do you understand? That's what you say and *I* say. Agreed?' She patted the back of his hand twice, three times.

Roger nodded. His confidence was creeping back, some of the feeling he had had yesterday, and many days before yesterday, that his decision was a right one, even if a private decision. Now it seemed a family decision.

'That's what I'll tell Joe . . . at least for now, Pop, that she fell down the stairs. She didn't deserve to live on . . . after you, Pop.'

Nil by Mouth, Inspector Ghote

H R F Keating

Inspector Ghote ought, as he entered the guarded Cabin No. 773 in the big noisy hospital, to have looked first of all at the criminal lying on the bed there, his kneecap shattered. But, instead, his eye was caught for some reason by the boldly printed card fastened to the top of the white tubular iron bed-head. 'Nil by Mouth' it said in thick black capitals in English, with below in devanagri script the same warning repeated in more immediately comprehensible terms 'No food or drink allowed'.

He turned to the Sister, neat in her starched white head-dress and white overall with smart epaulettes, its cotton belt fastened with a wide metal buckle. 'Please,' he said, 'what for is it that he is not allowed food. Is it on police orders? We are wanting him to talk, you know.'

The Sister looked shocked.

'No, no,' she said. 'This man is a patient in hospital, whatever he may have done outside. Here it is Resident Medical Officer's orders that count only. Patient is in Nil by Mouth condition because operation is to take place at six pip emma today.'

She turned away and stamped out, as if to re-emphasise that here within hospital walls it was the medical staff who gave orders, not any policewalla.

And then Ghote looked at the man he had come to see, had come to interrogate. Ram Dharkar, small-time goonda. But small-time muscleman who worked for a very, very big-time gang boss, the mystery man believed to be behind twenty-five well-organised bank dacoities in the past nine months. The man no one in Crime Branch had been able to get near.

But now, thanks to Ram Dharkar, they stood a chance. Because Dharkar had been found only five or six hours ago lying unconscious on a rubbish heap near the foul-smelling Chandanwadi Electric Crematorium, with his right knee smashed to pieces by a heavy lump of concrete left bloodily beside him. A clear case of a supposed informer having been punished and left as a lesson for any other gang member or hanger-on who might be thinking greedily of the large reward the banks of Bombay had, at last, collaborated to offer.

And the beauty of it was that Ram Dharkar had not been an informer at all. So, rightly aggrieved, he ought to be ready to talk and talk.

Ghote, who had been waiting for him to recover consciousness, sitting for hours down in the crowded echoing entrance hall of the big hospital on a hard bench underneath a strident notice saying 'OPD Case Notes Will Be Issued From 7.30 am' – whatever that meant – had now at last been given the news by a white-capped ward-boy that Dharkar was in a condition to be interviewed.

He then followed the boy through long clackingly shrill corridors, up one wide stone-stepped staircase and down another, to a nursing station where he had been handed over to the starchy Sister who had taken him to Cabin No.

773 and Ram Dharkar, Ram Dharkar surely ready to talk, lying helpless on the bed within.

'Well, Ram,' Ghote said to him, 'you and I know each other of old, isn't it?'

The goonda on the bed made no reply, eyeing Ghote sullenly though wakefully.

'And how are you feeling?' Ghote asked, showing as much friendly concern as he could. 'The knee, it is giving pain, no?'

Again Ram Dharkar did not respond.

Ghote pulled up a sagging-seated grey canvas chair he had spotted in a corner by the little room's sole narrow window. He sat himself down and leaned towards the injured man, who was, true enough, looking as if he was in not a little pain.

'Right then,' he said, 'let us be getting down to business. The Dada of your gang decided you were betraying one and all, isn't it? Well, we are damn well knowing such is not so. And the Dada, whoever he is, ought to be knowing as much also. Ram Dharkar was never a kabari.'

He looked for some sign of stirred pride in the goonda's lined face.

But there was nothing. Only that same sullen single expression.

He cleared his throat a little.

'No,' he said, feeling the falsity of the note of cheerfulness he was endeavouring to inject into his voice. 'No, that fellow should have known you better, Ram bhai. And look what he was doing to you instead. They tell me that however well is going the operation you are soon to have you will find difficulty to walk for the rest of your life.'

No reaction.

Ghote sat and thought.

This he had not expected. The situation had seemed to him quite straightforward. The Dada behind the bank dacoities had made a mistake, his first and only mistake, but a big one. He had had Ram Dharkar cruelly punished for something he had not at all done. So, surely, Ram Dharkar would be avid for revenge. And revenge was there. He knew, he must know, who the Dada was and where he could be found. He had only to say and his chance to pay back the man who had had him crippled would be one hundred per cent secured.

But here the fellow was, obstinately silent. Saying nothing.

Ghote's glance fell again on the bed-head notice. 'Nil by Mouth.' Yes, that was what Ram Dharkar was so unexpectedly giving him, nil by mouth. Absolutely nil.

But why? Why?

And then he thought he had it.

'You are afraid?' he asked the goonda abruptly. 'Afraid, if you are talking, the Dada will finish off the job he was beginning?'

Ram Dharkar still did not reply. But his expression of stony nothingness changed. His eyes said yes.

'But that is not so,' Ghote assured him eagerly. 'Think, man, where you are. You are in one of the biggest hospitals in Bombay. You are in a cabin on your own. There is a constable on guard just outside that door. He has orders to let in just only two nurses and one doctor. You cannot be more safe.'

He thought then, from the faintly pensive expression on Ram Dharkar's face, that he had taken all this in and was at least considering it.

But, no.

'Inspector, I do not dare.'

The words were croaked out. Yet Ghote took heart
from them. At least the fellow was communicating. With
patience and luck, he might be persuaded before long
that it was safe to take the revenge that lay so easily in his
power, as surely it was. The chances of any gang
executioner sent by the Dada getting to his possible
betrayer were a hundred to one against. More, even.

And almost at once Ram Dharkar showed that he had
committed himself to more than that one negative
sentence.

'Inspectorji,' he said, his voice a little stronger. 'Get us
a drink, no? I am thirsty-thirsty like hell.'

Ghote looked at the Nil by Mouth notice. 'Oh, I cannot
do that, man,' he said. 'You are having operation soon
and it is medical advice that you must take nothing
before.'

'But a drink only. A little water. Inspectorji, it is damn
hot in here. I am wanting just only one swallow of water.
That cannot be doing any harm.'

Ghote wondered whether this in fact might not be true.
Surely a single gulp of pure water would not make the
operation due in five hours' time altogether dangerous?

He looked around the narrow cabin. But there was no
jug of water or earthenware chatti to be seen. And, sure
enough, the little room was appallingly hot.

'Well,' he said, glancing at the door, 'perhaps . . .'

But at that moment the door was pushed open and the
two nurses presumably permitted to enter came in,
wheeling a small trolley consisting of a padlocked metal
chest on a stand.

'Dharkar, Ram,' said the more senior of the two.
'Medication has been ordered.'

She took a key from the bunch at her waist and
solemnly unlocked the metal chest. Ghote saw that its

interior was lined with pill bottles and jars by the dozen. The nurse consulted a sheet of paper and then selected one of the bottles.

'Excuse me,' Ghote said, prompted by a lingering resentment at the way the medical staff assumed that they and they only had a God-given right to do what they wanted when they wanted. 'Excuse me, but isn't it that this man is in Nil by Mouth condition?'

The nurse turned towards him, eyes sparking. 'Are you saying we do not know our duty?' she snapped. 'Tests have been carried out. Patient is not fit for immediate operation. The heart rate must be brought down.'

She turned to her colleague, showing her the label on the pill bottle.

'Digoxin two hundred and fifty micrograms,' she said.

'Digoxin two hundred and fifty micrograms,' the other nurse confirmed.

'One every four hours.'

'One every four hours.'

The senior nurse poured a little water from a vacuum flask in the medicine chest into a small plastic glass, handed Ram Dharkar a single white pill and the glass and watched him swallow the pill down.

When the pair of them had left, Ghote turned to the injured goonda again.

'Well,' he said, 'you have had your taste of water, after all.'

'And it is making it bloody worse,' Ram Dharkar responded. 'It is like giving a starving man one corner of a sweetmeat only.'

'Well,' Ghote answered, 'I suppose you must endure it. They did not take away that notice above your head.'

'But, Inspectorji, it is hot-hot. Feel only how hot I am.'

Ghote bent forward and took the goonda's calloused hand. It was thickly wet with sweat.

'Yes,' he said. 'Yes, you are hot. Even I am also.'

He glanced round the little room. Not even a fan to be seen.

'I tell you what,' he said. 'I would see if I can open that window.'

He got up and went across to the narrow, opaque-glass affair. For a moment he wondered whether he had been sensible to make the offer. With the window open, could Ram Dharkar, afraid for his life, make his escape through it should he himself have to leave the guarded cabin before he had finally got hold of that name? The fellow might think of it. He might. And then they would have lost their one golden opportunity.

But that was nonsense. Dharkar with his smashed kneecap would be totally incapable of getting through a window as narrow as this.

He thrust up its lower frame.

But nevertheless, having done so, he could not prevent himself putting his head out and making a careful survey of the escape possibilities.

No, he decided after a long look round, it really was safe enough. True, the window did overlook a lane inside the huge hospital compound. But, though technically at ground-floor level, it was in fact quite high up. A beggar, or some such, sitting crouched against the wall below, a piece of gunny laid out beside him to collect alms, looked from above quite small, his dirty-haired head like a dried coconut with the stump of one out-thrust leg – the fellow must be a leper, perhaps a patient from another department – looking like one of the flat bats dhobis used to beat washing clean. There was, certainly, a drainpipe running up the wall nearby, and an active man could probably scramble down that to the ground. But Ram Dharkar was the very opposite of an active man. No, it was safe enough.

Ghote turned from the window. Air less humidly hot than that in the room did seem to be drifting in.

'Better, heh?' he said to Ram Dharkar. 'Cooler, no?'

The goonda grunted unwilling assent.

'But all the same,' he said, 'I am wanting-wanting something to drink.'

'Well, we would be seeing about that perhaps later,' Ghote answered with vague helpfulness. 'But now. Now let us talk about the man who had that done to your knee.'

'No.'

'But . . .'

'No, no, Inspectorji. I tell you he is not a person to be playing with, that one. If he had one idea only that I had given his name, or that I was thinking only – why, if he knew I was just only talking with you now – then it would be the finish of me straightaway.'

'But think, man. How could he do that? When you are here, police guarded, in this hospital?'

'I am not knowing how. But I am knowing that he would do it.'

'But revenge. You could be taking revenge for what he has just done. Give us his name only, and where we could find, and in one hour, in one half-hour, he would be behind the bars and you, you would be here laughing.'

But Ram Dharkar merely turned his head away and lay silent.

Ghote sat on his uncomfortably sagging chair beside the bed and tried to think of some new line to take. But he felt that with every passing minute his chances of catching on to the injured goonda's desire for revenge – and, surely, surely he had that – were getting less.

At last the fellow stirred and gave a weary moan.

'So hot,' he said.

'Yes, it is hot. And if it had not been for your Dada you would not be here sweating it out, in pain, and on a crutch for the rest of your life also. So what is his name, man? What is his name?'

'A drink. I would give anything for one good, long, cool drink. Thandai, Inspector. You are knowing thandai?'

'Yes,' Ghote answered, trying for a new bond of sympathy. 'When I was a young man often I was taking thandai at that place at Kalba Devi where they are making specially. And very good it was, that milk, the ice crushed in and the mixed flavours, almond, pistachio, rose water, melon seeds. Oh, yes.'

'And, Inspectorji, something else also?' The injured goonda's voice had taken on a note of girlish coyness.

'Ah,' Ghote said, with a little laugh. 'The bhang that fellow is putting in sometimes, eh? The stuff that sends you into a nice, nice dream.'

'That is it, Inspector. That is it. Ah, what would I not give at just only this moment for a long, long drink of bhang thandai.'

And then an idea came into Inspector Ghote's head, an altogether wrong idea. But an idea of insidious appeal.

For a while he fought it down. He tackled Ram Dharkar once more, putting to him again all the arguments he had offered before. He could think of no others. But all his efforts seemed to be wasted. The goonda lay there on the bed, his face blankly inexpressive, occasionally letting out almost against his will a groan of pain and frustration.

Then, brutally interrupting, right in the middle of one of Ghote's most complex, and most persuasive, sentences, the fellow spoke again. 'Oh, shut up, shut up,' he said. 'What for are you going on and on? There is one thing only I am wanting, that bhang thandai. That only.'

And Ghote succumbed.

'Very well,' he said. 'If I am going out and smuggling in for you as big a drink of thandai as you have ever seen in your life, will you in exchange give me that name?'

The offer certainly got to the injured goonda. Ghote could positively see him swallowing down in anticipation that long, cool, refreshing and peace-bringing drink.

And, he thought, damn it all, that nurse said the operation had been delayed. So what real harm could there be in letting the fellow have something solid to drink? They must have left that Nil by Mouth card up there by mistake. He was not really endangering the man's life by letting him have his thandai.

And, when it came to it, he could always get the name out of him first and then throw the drink out of the window.

But would the fellow accept the offered bribe? Would he?

'Big-big? Double size?'

The bait had been taken. Right or wrong, it was to be done now.

And, perhaps, when he got back – getting the stuff was going to take him some little time – that notice would have been removed from the bed-head and Ram Dharkar would be able to have as much 'by mouth' as he liked. And if bhang would hardly be permitted by the hospital authorities, it would not do the fellow much harm. Might even do good, ease the pain.

'All right, my friend, I am off now. About half an hour, a little more perhaps. And you be thinking what you would be telling, no? Every detail you are able to remember. Then there will be no mistake in nabbing that Dada of yours.'

In fact, it took Ghote rather more than an hour to complete his errand. He realised first that he would need a good container to get the stuff into Ram Dharkar's cabin unobserved, something that would fit into his own briefcase. That took him some time to find amid the high-piled shops of Lohar Chawl with their heaps of crockery and glassware in orderly mounds, their bright plastic buckets piled in man-high towers, their steel or alumin-ium glasses in carefully constructed pyramids, their electric hot-plates and toasters tempting the middle classes and the pushing, gawping crowds buying and not buying, beating down prices and paying too much.

But at last he found a flat plastic flask with a screw top that looked as if it would hold a really sizeable amount of cooling thandai. Then he had to hurry down to Kalba Devi where the specialist in thandai had his stall. And there, since the day was scorchingly hot, he found a long, slow-moving line of customers waiting to be served and had patiently to stand in it till he reached its head. He even had some trouble then persuading the thandaiwalla, cross-legged on a small bench beneath his cupboard-like, bright pink-painted stall to pour the concoction into his plastic container, though one quick whispered word and the sight of a twenty-rupee note had sufficed to get him a mixture well laced with bhang.

Hurrying back to the hospital, Ghote began to worry that he might somehow be too late. Of course Ram Dharkar must still be there. That was one certain thing. The fellow could not move. But might he have somehow changed his mind? Might some thought of how the mysterious Dada could get at him despite all precautions have made him determined after all not to say one more single word?

Or could he, in the past hour, somehow have received

a warning from the Dada? But how? No, it was impossible. A vision of a paper dart being flown in through that narrow open window momentarily crossed his mind. But that was ridiculous. Utter fantasy.

The constable on guard at the cabin's door being bribed to let someone in just long enough to deliver a threat? Well, it was possible. But he himself knew the fellow, a man near retirement, two yellow long-service stripes on his sleeve. As trustworthy as anybody in the force.

Nevertheless, entering the noisy, crowded entrance hall of the hospital – 'OPD Case Notes', the letters must stand for Out Patients' Department, of course – he could not prevent himself from breaking into a walk not far short of a trot. Luckily he remembered how to get to Cabin No. 773, along one high, white-tiled corridor, his footsteps tapping out, up a wide set of stairs, along again, the white tiles here cracked and sometimes splashed with rust-red betel-juice stains, down another staircase, past the nursing station, briefcase with its illegal guggling flask inside, a quick nod to the Sister on duty, and there he was, outside Cabin No. 773, the grey-haired long-serving constable squatting beside its door scrambling up to salute him, alert as ever.

'No trouble, Constable?'

'No trouble, Inspector.'

And in. And there was Ram Dharkar lying on the bed, looking as if he had hardly moved in the past hour.

Looking, in fact, a good deal worse, Ghote thought, than when he had left him. But an hour more of pain, that would probably account for the clouded eyes, the yet greyer complexion. And the sight and smell of refreshing thandai – it ought still to be noticeably cool – should surely revive him.

'Well, man,' he said, infusing his voice with enthusiasm, 'thandai I have got. A big-big lot, more than you have ever had before, I am betting.'

He unscrewed the top of the flask and held it just under Ram Dharkar's grey, unmoving face.

And got no response. No response at all.

He swirled the scented pink liquid in the flask and held it near the sick man again.

'Take, take,' he said. 'Take one good drink and then be telling me that name.'

But Ram Dharkar lay unmoving.

Damn it, had the fellow gone right back to the beginning again? Had he, in that past hour, decided once more that he dared not speak? Not despite every precaution taken to guard him? Not despite his own promise to have the Dada nabbed within half an hour of learning his name and whereabouts? Not despite this offered illegal bribe?

Now suddenly, without warning, the goonda lying flat on the bed began to vomit.

Ghote was appalled. This was something he had not at all expected. And the fellow, he realised now, looked desperately ill. On the point of death even.

He tore across to the door of the little room, flung it open, saw with relief a nurse trotting down the corridor outside – it was the Sister who had first shown him where the cabin was – and shouted to her that Ram Dharkar was very, very ill.

In a moment she was beside the vomiting goonda's bed making a quick, professional analysis.

'Yes,' she said, 'he is serious. Very serious. Ring that bell, Inspector. We are going to need much more of help if he is not to expire.'

Ghote rang the bell, cursing himself for not having realised it was there before, and then retreated to the farthest corner of the narrow room while two other nurses and, soon, a doctor came on to the scene.

He watched, caught in horrified fascination, while they worked to save the dying man. And thoughts, grim thoughts, ran through his mind.

Ram Dharkar had been poisoned. He was sure of it, if only from what he gathered from the terse questions and answers of the team round the bed. And if the fellow had been poisoned, then it was almost certain who was behind it. The Dada. The mysterious gang boss whose name he himself had counted on learning just a few minutes earlier. Somehow, he thought, word must have got back to this unknown master criminal that a Crime Branch inspector had been closeted with the injured so-called informer for a considerable period. And the man had acted. Had acted with all the speed and decision with which the twenty-five bank dacoities he had planned had been carried out. He had, somehow, got poison into poor Ram Dharkar, and, it looked, in time to shut his mouth for ever before he had spoken his name.

But how? How on earth had it been managed?

Then, abruptly, Ghote thrust aside the almost useless question. Because through the leaning, busily working bodies of the nurses round the dying man he had caught a glimpse of Ram Dharkar's face. And his eyes, fixed on his own, had seemed to be attempting to tell him something.

Regardless of the urgent medical work around the bed, he advanced carefully towards it. And, yes, as he did so he was certain that Ram Dharkar was responding. If a look alone could do it, he was saying, Come, come, there is something I must tell.

Ghote got himself as close to the head of the bed as he could without actually impeding the nurse there. Ram

Dharkar's eyes were plainly now begging him to give him his utmost attention. Now, in all probability knowing himself to be dying, knowing that he had been poisoned – but how? How? – he was at last determined to take revenge and name the Dada.

But the only sound that came from his vomit-flecked mouth was a feeble croak. Ghote turned his head and strove to catch every nuance of the sound. The dying man croaked out a noise again. But this was yet feebler than the time before.

Was he never going to manage to say the one word, two perhaps, that would gain him even in death his revenge? Second by second it looked less and less likely. If ever the marks of death were on a face, for all the desperate efforts of the doctor and nurses, they were on Ram Dharkar's now.

Ghote felt a surge of pure anger. To have been defeated by his mysterious antagonist in this way. At the very last moment.

And how had the man managed it? How had he got someone with poison into the guarded room?

He leaned yet nearer the dying man, willing him and willing him into one last spurt of life, a moment of vigour just long enough to pronounce the name.

But not all his effort to hold Ram Dharkar in this world seemed to be helping. His eyes, clouded only until a few moments ago, now were plainly glazed over.

Then, suddenly, Ghote thought he knew how it had been done. The nurses. The nurses with the wheeled medicine chest. They must have been bribed. Or substitutes must have replaced them and somehow, perhaps merely by the swiftness with which they had entered, they had tricked the old constable on guard at the door. And that single little white pill he himself had seen them administer, that must have been the poison. No wonder they had not taken away the Nil by Mouth notice. They had given the would-be betrayer all that was needed 'by mouth' to silence him for ever.

His mind raced. Perhaps after all he did not need to hear the name which, it was clear now, Ram Dharkar was never going to be able to pronounce. It was possible, surely, that the two false nurses, or the two bribed nurses, could be traced. Traced, arrested and interrogated. Interrogated, however toughly was necessary, until they squeaked. And, if not able to name the mastermind Dada directly, be persuaded into giving enough information about who had given them their evil task, wittingly or unwittingly performed, for the trail to lead eventually to that mysterious lurking figure. It needed only one end of the thread to be in police hands and they could be sure, very nearly sure, of getting to the Dada.

He was so excited by his discovery, wondering even whether he should leave the little room and the dying goonda at once and begin enquiries about the nurses with the medicine chest, that he almost failed to notice a change that had come about in the man on the bed.

But he did notice. His attention had been so riveted upon him up to this instant that its residue was enough to alert him.

Plainly, Ram Dharkar's last moments had come. A deep agitation was passing through him.

And then, although speech was evidently beyond him, his final convulsion of energy did produce something that until now he had seemed incapable of.

The dying man sat up. And, teetering precariously, he flung out his right arm in a gesture of pointing. The forefinger was rigid as a rod of steel. And he was pointing, in a manner that could not be denied, at the

70

narrow window of the little room, the window still open at the bottom from when Ghote himself had tried to bring in a little cooler air.

Ghote looked at the window, looked back at Ram Dharkar. And saw in the hope in the man's now momentarily clearer eyes that he himself had begun to read correctly his last message.

There was more of it, too. With a supreme effort, keeping his gaze fixed on Ghote's face, the dying goonda made another gesture. He bunched the fingers of the hand that had pointed so dramatically at the window into a tight knot.

A knot that at once reminded Ghote of something. For a long moment his mind battered against the answer like a dull fly battering at a window pane. And then he had it. A leper. Ram Dharkar's hand was unmistakably imitating the fingerless stump of a leper.

A leper. The leper. The leper he himself had seen, and had discounted, squatting beneath that very window. The leper, or more likely the imitation leper, who must have listened, keen-eared, to every word that had passed between Ram Dharkar and himself. The man who must have heard the promise of a drink of thandai and who, acting with speed and decision – why, yes, yes, he must be, he could only be the Dada himself in disguise – had hurried off, obtained some cool drink that looked enough like proper thandai and had then swarmed up the drainpipe outside, in the way he himself had envisaged Ram Dharkar, if he had had full use of his legs, swarming down and had then, keeping his face averted, offered the drink. The poisoned drink.

So, yes, at last from the dying man he had learned all that he had wanted to know. Had learned it nil by mouth.

Quietly Inspector Ghote withdrew from the poisoned

goonda's deathbed. Quietly he made his way over to the still open window. Carefully he poked his head out just far enough to catch one glimpse of the dried-coconut disguised head of the supposed leper crouching there waiting to know whether his daring plan had been successful.

The Dada himself. And, not knowing one thing. That his disguise had been penetrated. That he was now dangerously exposed. That the arms of the law were on the point of being able to enfold him. The Dada. The mastermind.

Quietly as ever Ghote climbed up till his hands were grasping the top of the window and his feet were on its bottom ledge. The gap would be just wide enough, he saw with grim pleasure, to slide his body through.

He launched himself.

Requiescat

Philip Kerrigan

The body lay unwashed on the bed where it had died.

A silent man waited on the hill above the house, poised behind the barrel of his rifle like a counterweight.

The one left alive sat in the cold parlour.

Old stone and the odour of damp; walls hung with mildewed pictures; smoke of the fire wafting back into the room; tiny windows permitting dirty handkerchiefs of light.

The body lay in the next room, face outlined by a spill of daylight.

The body in the next room.

The one left alive, a man of forty, sat alone before the choking fire. Eyes open, wetted by the smoke. Chin resting on one clenched hand. He rocked slowly back and forth. The chair creaked in its joints; his bones creaked in theirs. He stared into the flames. The fire gave him no heat. He rocked slowly, listened, thought.

Something dropped. Struck the roof over his head, tumbled down the slates and fell to the ground by the window. He heard a miniature scream. A kestrel, flying by some hundred feet above, had dropped its prey.

A harsh wind called to him under the front door, the only door to the outside. The fire sputtered. Though he never altered his position in the chair, he sought to calm himself. Deliberately forced himself to be calm. His knuckles turned from bone to flesh again.

Oh, God, he thought. I don't know how I can escape from this.

A breath of draught stirred a lock of hair on the body's face. Its blue eyes, clouded like the sky upon the hills, observed nothing. The room was stone, the body was becoming stone; the wound, congealed and hardened, was a growth of lichen in the stone.

The one left alive removed his chin from the support of his hand. He noticed flecks of crusted blood on the knuckles.

I'll reason with him, he thought. I'll speak to him and make him understand. I'll talk him out of this thing he wants to do.

He remembered the body next door, and knew it could not be done. Thought of the silent man on the hill, finger resting on the trigger. He would allow no explanations. Not after what had happened.

The body on the bed was recently deceased. The hair still grew from its lovely head, the nails still pushed out, a millimetre at a time, from the fine hands.

He rocked, and the sound of his rocking was loud in the stillness. The joints of the chair cracked and popped, the damp wood on the fire whined. Tongues of blue and green flared momentarily and sank.

There could be no end to this except the one he saw, as a picture reproduced in some official file, of his own figure, broken in some way that could not be repaired, lying just beyond the threshold.

He was afraid to move, although certain in his mind that the silent man on the hill had not changed his position. There was, after all, no need. From the nest of granite and heather, he could see the house and all the ground about it for a hundred yards.

One hundred yards, the one left alive thought. A ten-second dash for an athlete, not much more for a schoolboy or a man who is fit. Even I could run it in such a time.

But ten seconds over the even ground about the grey stone cottage was a spell of leisure for such as the silent man. How many rounds might he fire from his rifle in so many seconds? Enough, and more than enough.

He shivered again, wishing he had his coat. The coat was near, but he could not wear it.

The body lay as it had lain when the last breath of life was expelled. Except he had removed the dark and sodden towels from the wound. They lay beside the bed, stiff and caked. The coat the body wore was open around it. It had been too big in life, and seemed bigger now.

He bit down upon the back of his hand, tasting his own blood as he had tasted hers.

Oh, God, if only she hadn't put it on.

He recalled then her penchant for wearing others' clothes. With a crippled imitation of the smile which made him realise he was falling in love with her, he saw her as he had first seen her: at a party. He was talking to a prospective customer about racing yachts, when he saw a woman in a huge white shirt approaching.

The prospective customer knew her, introduced her.

All he could think to say – because even then he was captured by her – was: 'Where did you get that?'

She laid her hand on his arm. He still felt in the nerves of his body how the contact had shocked him with desire.

'Don't tell anyone.' She smiled. 'But I borrowed it from my husband.'

He was faintly disappointed, even then, at the mention of a husband. The conversation continued, fuelled by the wine of her vivacity, until he began to wonder where this lucky man might be.

It was late before he discovered she was alone. Her husband was in the Army. An officer. He could not imagine this bright woman married to the Army. And how could any man leave her for months at a time?

He did not realise at first how deeply she lodged in him. He was working hard, and already had the debts of a bad marriage to pay by monthly instalments. He did not play with married women, having been to some extent the victim of another who did. He could honestly swear that she did not cross his mind for a month after they met.

Yet the perfume of her flesh and the curve of her lips when she smiled were inside him, and he dreamed her body several times without consciously knowing it was her.

The body that lay on the bed beneath the weather-scoured roof. No laughter now, no joy in being.

He met her again: by chance, of course. At the Boat Show, where his company had a stand.

'So this is what you do,' she declared, coming towards him through the crowd. She wore a man's white jacket. He did not need to ask where it came from. Under the brilliant lighting, she seemed more real than anyone else. She glittered.

'What brings you here?' he said.

'Oh, we used to sail when I was a child. My father had a little skiff on the lakes. Besides, my husband likes them. He should be in the Navy!'

The husband, it became clear, was there also. After a few minutes, he appeared from the throng. A big and silent man who allowed his wife to shine the more for his quietness. His face was a mask of taut flesh. He spoke few words, obviously uninterested in anything they had to say.

'You must come down to my boat some weekend,' the grey-haired man said to the couple, as he said it to many people in the course of a week, expecting nothing more than their polite but insincere acceptance.

He travelled home that night with music playing loud and strong on the car stereo. He wondered what kind of relationship the couple had; the woman so bright, the man so quiet. Found himself trying to guess at their lovemaking. Her eyes were full of light, her voice chimed in his memory. He was already in love, although he did not know it.

Eyes dulled now, watching and not watching. She had died staring at him, and he had remained for a long time after, at first unsure, then – when he knew – studying in an empty, half-conscious way, the life drain from her.

A fortnight, this time, before he saw her again. The endless grind of business, meetings all day long. That weekend, he went down to his own sloop as usual. Not to sail so much as to be on the water with wide skies overhead, and to sleep in peace for two nights.

She arrived Saturday morning; appearing on the jetty in the gleam of spring sunlight, dressed casually, acting casual. But he knew.

'I was out driving,' she said. 'I remembered your invitation.'

He watched her from the deck. Green water slapped between hull and jetty. 'And your husband?' he asked.

'Abroad again,' she said.

He put out his hand to her. She came aboard.

Up on the hill, beneath a thin prickle of rain, the silent man shifted slightly. He squinted against the rain. He levelled the rifle once more. Waited.

'It was so simple.' The words, spoken in the silence of the parlour, stopped his rocking. He braced his feet against the floor, gazing into the fire. Its flames were sinking, the ashes glowed. 'Why does a thing simple and pure have to end like this?'

He stood up, amazed that he could do this much. The room's walls and floor and ceiling bent and pitched, perspectives changing with his movement. He shamed himself by avoiding the windows as he crossed the room.

I should not care now, he thought. Not with the body of his love spread out upon the counterpane next door.

He approached the door. The solid oak planks were locked and barred; the walls were a foot thick. He edged sideways, glanced out. The tiny panes showed a stretch of levelled earth, in the middle of which was the car.

He touched the keys in his pocket.

If I could just distract him, he thought. If I could get his attention away for a few seconds. He considered a dash to the car. How many seconds would that take? Open the door, fool the silent man somehow, then flat out for the car no more than ten yards away. Once there, he would be concealed by the car's body. He might be able to get the door open and drive away without being hit.

The man on the hill could not be distracted. He could not be fooled.

I must think of something.

The silent man on the hill stared unblinking at the house. The rifle was steady.

That first Sunday, after they had spent the night aboard, she brought him coffee, wearing one of his Arran sweaters. She was totally his, he thought, no one else's.

The husband was, first and ever after, a nebulous figure to him. Pale knowledge came with many other fragments he collected in their succeeding afternoons and nights together. She hardly ever made a deliberate point of talking about him, but a sentence or two now and then filtered through the gauze of his infatuation, serving only to confirm what his jealousy originally whispered: the husband was a brutal man; he had no soul with which to appreciate anything beyond her physical beauty; he was insensitive to the obvious yearning for a spiritual poetry inside her.

'Why don't you leave him?' he asked one time, before he had seriously thought of it. She looked scared, and he almost laughed, because surely no woman these days *had* to fear a husband's wrath?

'He wouldn't allow it,' she said.

Then he did laugh, kissed her, not believing.

It was only as the affair grew more sweet and painful to him that he realised she meant it. He came to understand, although not really believe, that she existed in a kind of animal terror. He no longer remembered when he first learned more about the husband's job. He was not, it seemed, regular Army; he belonged to some special group. When quizzed, she was vague.

'It's not the SAS,' she said. 'I don't know what he really does.'

He knew the man was strong, that something danger-ous lived behind his mask of a face. But he did not contemplate going up against such a man. There was no need for that, he reasoned. Not these days.

These ideas crowded in on him when next the husband came home on leave. It was impossible to see her for a month, and the weeks were almost unbearable. At first, he threw himself into work, slept badly, drank too much. Then, while lunching with a client one day, he actually saw them together. They ate at a corner table, exchanging monosyllables, while the husband kept his eye on the room.

After that, he could not eat or sleep, nor give his mind to anything else. He was tortured by visions of her in the arms of her husband, saw her wearing the husband's dressing gown as she padded downstairs to make them coffee.

When the husband was gone once more, he sought her out and told her she must leave him. He was as serious as he had ever been, as undeniable as the tides.

She cried. She told him she wanted it too, but it could not happen. Her husband . . .

'Your husband,' he said, 'doesn't love you. He wouldn't leave you for months on end if he loved you.' At that moment, he truly believed what he said.

They wept and fought most of that weekend. Both stretched far beyond any limits they had ever thought themselves capable of. He was wrought to a pitch he had never experienced, but felt himelf to be fully in control, strong with his passion.

Oh, God, he thought, leaving the useless vision of the car and returning to the rocking chair. If only there were a phone, or a house nearby to call to. He sat down, rocked back. One telephone call would end it. One call.

Finally she agreed. He felt bad at first, as if he had battered her into submission. But when they made love, she was his again, and her eagerness convinced him he was right to do as he had; never understanding that her actions were those of one who knew all further time was borrowed, and had accepted it.

'How?' she asked. 'How do we go about this?'

He suggested they wait until her husband returned from duty, then face him with the news. No questions or answers. Just plain, cold fact, like immovable stone.

The stones of the fireplace black with soot, the walls transmitting an outer cold.

No, she said. It could not be that way. She could not live so long with the fear and the waiting. 'I can't face him,' she said. 'We have to go away where he can't touch us. Then he'll have time to get used to it. Maybe then . . .' The sentence hung unfinished like cigarette smoke in an empty room.

He took her in his arms. 'Darling,' he said. 'This is the twentieth century. You're free to leave him if you want to. He can't do anything to us.'

'No,' she said, but was adamant: if they were to do it, it must be now.

Together they wrote letters to the husband; one from her, one from him. They wrote many drafts, trying to explain themselves.

Thinking of that now, he sighed at his naïvety. To believe that explaining his side of things would make the silent man sympathetic.

They brought the letters to perfection, then held them for several days while he made preparations to go. Without consciously considering it, he gave her several of his shirts and sweaters while he was away from her, insisting that she wear them. Her own manner had infected him to a degree where he believed in talismans and symbols such as these. He placed his company in the hands of his managing director; he opened new bank accounts; he found the converted crofter's hut in the Highlands. It was miles from the nearest village, possessed no phone. A loch nearby would provide them with sailing if they wished it. They would affirm their love in

81

simplicity, secure in the knowledge that no one knew their whereabouts.

It must have been Joseph, he thought, for the first time. His feet scuffed on the floor. He had given the address to his director, in case something very urgent came up. Christ, I shouldn't have given him that.

The silent man on the hill checked his watch.

The body lay on the bed.

At the end of that week they were ready. He went to her house, persuaded her once more that all would be well, that her husband would not do anything. He was happy and confident, secure in the knowledge that the twentieth century is a good age for married lovers. The cuckold no longer has recourse to physical action for revenge; he must live by the law, and do the lovers damage only through the courts.

'Come,' he said, kissing away her tears. 'In a year from now, you won't remember why you were so afraid of him.'

He put her in the car, loaded it with the few belongings she wished to take, and they set off. As they left town, he stopped the car on a corner and posted the letters.

'That's it,' he told her. 'All finished.'

Not finished. He rocked steadily. The fire shrank further from him. Mostly smoke.

The first three weeks. He could not believe how happy he had been. Three weeks of early autumn: misty, cold mornings on the water, teaching her how to handle the skiff; afternoons lying together in bed; evenings of quiet pleasures. They read aloud to each other from poetry books – a thing he had not done since childhood. The bare green hills and the silver metal of the loch held them. Once, in the night, he found her standing by the window, staring out like a frightened child. She had woken from a dream; he soon quieted her. Three weeks that seemed far away and long past.

They had ended this morning at nine-fifteen.

The night had been windy and live with stars. Vast drifts of rain massed and glided over the hills without breaking, the loch was set to tossing like the sea. In the morning they woke early, listened to the world rushing above them.

She moved into the crook of his arm, rested her head on his shoulder.

'I love this place,' she said.

'So do I. Because of you.'

They had drifted into the motions of love then. He remembered her raised above him, trembling silently.

Dead now. Still for ever now.

They had breakfast. He lit the fire and began to cook bacon and eggs. The rich smell of coffee filled the kitchen.

'I could use a cigarette,' he said, as she slipped by him in nothing but sandals.

She frowned. She had been trying to make him cut down on his smoking. 'They're in the car,' she said.

'I'll get them.'

'No.' She smiled. 'You carry on with breakfast. I want to look at the morning anyway.'

And she went to the door.

'Don't go out like that,' he called. 'You'll frighten the birds.'

He saw her now in memory, turning back, body tight and curved, nipples erect from the cold. She gave him a strange look.

'Prude,' she said, and took his coat from the hanger by the door.

He watched her from the stove. 'You look better in it than I ever did.'

'I look just like you.' She grinned, posing for him.

'Not quite,' he murmured.

'Back in a minute,' she said, and opened the door.

Just like him.

He felt heat on his fingers. He was blind. It took a moment for him to understand that his hands were at his face, covering it as tears fell. He removed them, letting the dark grate and the wall come back into focus as he blinked the tears away.

Of course, it was a dreadful mistake. The deep, ragged scream that overlay the gunshot from the hill as she sprawled back across the threshold told him that. From up there, with only a moment to aim and shoot, it must have looked like him coming out of the doorway. Very likely the silent man, filled with his terrible love and the ability to draw revenge from an earlier day, realised what he had done in the instant when the bullet was leaving the barrel. But by then it was too late; it is impossible to take back a shot to the heart.

The stupidity of it. He had believed no harm could come to them, ignoring the fact that the husband was of another breed and time from any man he had ever met. Whatever job he did, it made this thing possible.

When the shock had dulled enough for him to contemplate the situation, when he had carried her broken body from the door to the bed and watched her die, he made an attempt to leave the house. The rifle barked again, and fragments leaped off the doorstep to slash at him. After that, he remained in the house, scraped and hollowed out by what he had seen.

He had expected then that the silent man would come down and finish him. It seemed only natural. But the minutes dragged into an hour and he was still alive. Perhaps, he thought, the shock had frozen the silent man too. Or perhaps he wished to draw out the agony before death. It hardly mattered. His position was perfect; and, this way, he had no need to come closer to the place where he had ended his love's existence.

He almost felt sympathy for the silent man, now that she was as silent as he.

We are not of the same world, he thought, flexing his hands to reduce the creeping numbness. I have lived all my life in a world that says such straightforward answers are no longer permissible. There is the law, and there is 'civilised behaviour'. Such things as this do not, are not allowed to, happen.

'Whereas you . . .' He lifted his head as if to speak to the silent man with whom he was at last united in grief. 'You move on the dark side of everything I've made real. God knows what you've seen and done that you can contemplate this as a fitting end, as a solution.'

The fire flickered away and died. Its silence met his own as he ceased rocking. Sunlight faded from the windows. The gloom in the parlour thickened. He was more aware of her, lying in the next room with her beauty intact like the petals of a rose after the stem is cut. It would not remain so for long, but he knew now that he would not be there to see its destruction.

It is impossible to wait him out, he thought. If I should stay here a hundred years, he will be there, waiting for me.

The silent man was of the hillside and the glen, the brutality of rock and earth; while they had clung to it for a second, in the briefest shaft of sunlight, not understanding that by taking flight into its lonely glory, they were placing themselves in his domain.

The wind mumbled under the door. It brushed his ankes and caressed his face with frigid love. Now he was paralysed, knowing that the only truth in the wasteland of her death was to be found by facing the silent man, giving himself the chance that was no chance, and the silent man opportunity to bring peace to all but himself. The insidious draught mocked his realisation. He was feeling what she already felt, and the silent man on the hillside would wait forever to keep their rendezvous.

The body on the bed in the chill, dank room; the grey-haired man before the lost fire, praying for the courage to act one final time; the house like a tombstone amid the green.

And the rifle waiting like a loving friend, to send its message across the drizzling air.

Teacher's Pet

Roger Longrigg

'I want you to draw the spaces *between* things,' said Miss Calloway the teacher, whom I later ventured to call Dorothea.

The five of us who were beginners in the Art Class obediently peered at the jumble of upturned kitchen stools she had arranged for us. I sharpened my HB pencil, uncovered a new sheet of cartridge paper, and made sure that my India rubber was ready to hand.

We had drawn a hand, a head and a bowl. Dorothea was frank about the purpose of these preliminary exercises – they enabled her to tell, quickly and economically, if any of us could draw at all, if we had had any training, if we showed obvious, conspicuous talent.

Frankly, I did.

I had had no formal training (when I was a schoolboy, to be 'arty' was to be a pariah) but it had been my habit to 'doodle' during meetings at the Ministry, and some of my colleagues – my most junior colleagues, I am glad to remember – chuckled appreciatively at my disrespectful renderings of the noses and poses of their seniors. I suspected one young fellow of forming a collection of my sketches, and somewhat regretted that I had not saved them myself. I did not then know about drawing the 'spaces between things'.

Retirement brought empty days. Though I had moved to the country, it was to a flat over the garage of my niece's house. I had no garden of my own, and no taste for pulling the bindweed out of my niece's gooseberries. I kept out of their way as much as I could. I was a quiet and careful tenant. When they came back from dinner parties on Saturday evenings, the clang of the garage doors almost knocked me out of bed. They expected a consideration they did not extend. They were charging me a small rent. I shopped and cooked for myself, but these things did not fill my days.

It was my nephew Nigel – to be exact, my niece's husband – who first told me about the Adult Education facilities provided, at a fee, by the County Council. It was an area of government remote from that in which I had spent the whole of my working life, and I did not even know where to write. Such matters were discovered for me, I think in the village shop, including the fact – no less welcome for being predictable – that as a pensioner I could attend at half the normal fee.

I did not then realise that nearly all the 'pupils' were pensioners; this, too, should have been predictable, since the class was on Tuesday mornings. It was quite abnormal to pay the 'normal' fee, the only persons doing so, as I speedily perceived, being young wives whose children were at school.

I approached the first lesson, on a blowy morning in late September, with a certain and absurd trepidation. I was too old and – dare I say it? – too eminent to feel like a 'new boy'. I was equipped only with a drawing-pad from our village shop, some pencils, an India rubber, a penknife. I expected to be taught the mysteries of paint-tubes, brushes, canvas, easel, palette, turpentine and so forth. I drove my small car to the market town of Mitchington, and, following the sketch-map provided by the Council, arrived a little early (ministerial habit holding) at the disused Infants' School.

Dorothea Calloway introduced herself boisterously. She was a gangling lady, her hair touched with grey, her spectacles flashing a zealous gleam, her clothes of the sort my niece would describe as 'ethnic'. She was in the middle of creating 'set-ups' for her more experienced pupils – arrangements on little tables of bottles, fruit, flowers. Some of the pupils had easels, some boards with bulldog clips, some little boxes full of bottles of ink, some great flat cases of pastels. Many had Thermos flasks. I was only surprised for a moment that their average age was greater than my own. They seemed to me awesomely professional, as they settled themselves with their impedimenta, and began at once conjuring *real pictures* out of the subjects they had chosen.

The beginners stood a little forlorn in the middle of all this expert bustle, until Dorothea Calloway addressed herself to finding out what sort of 'stuff we were made of'. This pause allowed me to inspect my fellows in the 'kindergarten', and gave them, no doubt, leisure to inspect me. They saw a man of average height, weight and shape (although sedentary years at desk and conference-table do not produce your lissomely active figure) with many of his own teeth and much of his hair, dressed approximately as for going shopping in a country town. (I foresaw with excitement, but had not yet ventured, a beret and a copious silk cravat.) They heard, but may not have absorbed, that my name is Harold

Love. I saw a sandy female in her fifties, an older female whose face had the appearance of being swollen by many insect bites, a girl in her twenties expecting, but not imminently, a baby which I guessed was her first, and John Bewley. His was the only name I caught. He was a few years older than myself; we stood chatting until our teacher had time for us; he had been a mining engineer, although he looked as though he had been assistant to an undertaker's mute. He had a little hair on a freckled skull; there was a touch of North Country in his voice. It was extremely surprising that this dim little man should nourish artistic ambitions. He seemed, himself, surprised to be at the class. I understood that he had been 'put up to it' by a younger relative.

With a flurry of hearty apology, Dorothea Calloway at last instructed us. She correctly assumed that we would all use pencils, that we had all brought paper. I seated myself. I contemplated my own left hand, and embarked on drawing it. Tricky, a hand! I made much use of my India rubber. The result was, not all at once, *like a hand*. I felt almost intoxicated, because it came to me that *I could draw*. I embarked with enthusiasm on a drawing of the head of the pregnant young woman. To catch a likeness is terribly difficult, not to be achieved all at once. I was pleased with the way I rendered the wave of her hair. After such challenges, the bowl seemed to me too easy. I shaded my drawing, delicately.

The sandy female's pencil squeaked as she laboriously drew and redrew the bowl. The older woman was breathing heavily as she blinked at her own hand, and made what I could see was a pathetically inept attempt at drawing it. The girl was quiet, intent. John Bewley, a little apart, seemed to have paper to burn; he scribbled on page after page of his ring-bound sketch-book, sometimes after

90

scratching in no more than a line or two.

Truly I felt sorry for them all. Unless their whole concern was to fill one morning a week, they were wasting their time here. I guessed that the experienced pupils I could see were the survivors of a much greater number, a majority having been brought to face the fact of their own lack of talent. I hoped, for the sake of their feelings, that the small ranks of my fellow beginners would thin rapidly and permanently.

I thought this thinning would be accelerated by the problem Dorothea Calloway now set us, that of 'drawing the spaces between' the legs and struts of those upturned stools. I attacked it with the kind of disciplined briskness for which I had been famous in the Department. My pencil conjured rhombus, trapezoid and triangle. The older woman moaned. John Bewley continued to make rapid and repeated false starts, the pages of his sketch-book aflutter.

The room was warm and brightly lit. There were murmurs of gossip, and of friendly comment when one artist paused to inspect the work of another. The atmosphere was delightful. I felt that a new and important door had opened in front of me. I foresaw a major interest, an abiding joy, and in time a corpus of work which would be hung with pride on many a discerning wall.

I admired Dorothea Calloway at the end of that first session. It would have been easy for her to have dismissed the work of the beginners as talentless, their presence here as purposeless. But she was careful to be encouraging, positive, about the work of all three women. She picked on this or that small error in their drawings. She said that experience would speedily put such mistakes behind them. She wanted them to come again.

With me she evidently realised that kindly lies were needless, would even be insulting. It was interesting to me – required by my erstwhile duties to make so many instant judgements of men, to pitch my voice and choose my words aptly for each different hearer – that this oddly dressed art teacher made so rapid and accurate a diagnosis. No comfortable fibs for *this* one, she told herself.

'It's a start,' was all she said to me, looking at my drawings. I knew that it was, indeed, and that for myself the future was limitless.

To John Bewley she adopted a different mode, one suggested by the kindness of her heart, and learned over her years of helping elderly fools through the boredom of retirement.

'*You*'ve been to an art school,' she said to him, flipping through his pages of scrawls. 'I think you're a fraud.'

'Never,' he said, with a senile giggle. 'Hardly put a pencil to paper in my life.'

Some of the experienced pupils, overhearing Dorothea Calloway's simulated amazement, came to look. As though drilled by their teacher, as though in a kindly conspiracy to bring happiness to the old man, they too threw up their hands, declared that he had been thoroughly and academically instructed, said that no one by instinct and intelligence alone could have produced such strong and fluent work. It was amusing and heart-warming to listen to them all, and to realise that this was the amiable custom of the place. The drawings themselves I barely saw, so great was the press of people about them, so manifestly worthless were they.

All the rest of that week I was pulled towards my own drawings, hand, head, bowl, stools, to stare and stare at them, to marvel at them and at myself for having created them. They seemed something quite outside myself, of which I had not dreamed myself capable.

After church on Sunday I lunched, as usual, with my niece and her husband. They demanded to see my drawings. I made the sort of modest show that is expected of an artist, and went at last to fetch them down from my garret over the garage.

'Oh, yes,' said he.

'My goodness,' said she.

They could not find other words. I understood, although other words would have been agreeable to me.

I told them – as an example of that very Christian charity about which the vicar had addressed us three hours before – the story of the warm-hearted conspiracy of teacher and class to cheer up a pathetic old man.

'And you saw his drawings?'

'Glimpsed them. They were what you'd expect.'

'Has it occurred to you, Harold,' said Nigel, 'that the old boy's drawings really were good?'

'Oh dear,' I said. 'You've entirely missed the point of the story.'

I was agog for my second lesson. I bought a larger block, of better paper. I wore a silk scarf instead of a tie.

The experts settled to their paints and pastels, and we beginners to an arrangement of cardboard boxes at various angles. The angles were the essence. We were taught to hold up a pencil, exactly horizontal or vertical, and so discover the steepness of the angles. I caught quickly on to this valuable technique. There were sounds of hard labour about me. John Bewley kept changing his position and embarking on new drawings, as though a different aspect would make it easier. It was distracting to have him bobbing up left, right and centre, and to hear the repeated squeak as he shifted his chair.

The comedy was played again. 'Most encouraging, you're getting the idea,' said Dorothea Calloway to each of the women. 'I suppose you must simply keep trying,' she said to me, which I was of course able to interpret as a more fervent encouragement than she would wish, in front of the others, to voice more explicitly. 'Actually, this is all quite incredible,' she said to John Bewley, who had done half a dozen drawings to my one, as though quantity made up for lack of quality. She spent only seconds with me; she spent five minutes with him. The experienced pupils, word perfect, expressed amazement and admiration as she raised the drawings for them to see.

'I suppose you must simply keep trying.' These words rang in my head. They were a call to me, of course. *Draw, draw,* develop this gift, give it to the world. And they were an account of my own spirit. I *must* keep trying. It was an internal as well as external imperative. On my little kitchen table I arranged pots and loaves and apples, conjuring subtleties of shape and shadow. I purchased a portfolio, and another and still larger block. I picked up, in the draper's shop in Mitchington, a blue beret; but I put it down again. 'By their works shall ye know them.' I had no need of badges.

Though I understood and applauded the intention, the amount of time Dorothea spent with John Bewley became vexing. She spoke to him about his scrawls with a seriousness which was wonderfully simulated, but at a length which was unfair to the rest of us. The women pretended not to mind. They pretended to be clamorously envious of John Bewley's 'talent' – they had caught the trick of the class. To me Dorothea used few words. I understood her understanding of the needlessness of effusion: but I would have appreciated the compliment of a more diligent scrutiny of my work.

I tried to show her all the drawings I had been doing at home. She scarcely spared them a glance. I thought her heart was ruling her head to a point which was becoming irresponsible.

After four lessons there was a 'half-term break', coincident, for some inscrutable bureaucratic reason, with that of the state schools. After the break, two of the beginners were seen to have dropped out, the pregnant girl and the elderly puffy-faced woman. It was no surprise and no loss. I had never discovered their names. John Bewley, sustained by fatuous deception and self-deception, eagerly re-presented himself. The sandy lady, now known to me as Isabel Craker, more shyly reappeared.

I saw, with tolerant derision, that John Bewley had promoted himself to a pen. Not a proper pen, with nib and ink bottle, but a kind of fancy foreign ballpoint. He had also acquired a new and pretentious kind of paper, something called 'Bockingford', expensive and for him absurd. I took it that the 'younger relative' of whom he had spoken had subsidised this folly.

I had filled the intervening fortnight with pencil studies of the 'fruits of the earth' from my niece's garden. 'Oh, yes,' my niece had said, pointing to a drawing of an apple – evocation, to my eyes, of the very essence of 'appleness' – 'I like the potato.' These things also are sent to try us.

'Oh, yes,' said Dorothea, as I opened my portfolio.

I knew that she meant – that she was conveying, almost in a secret language, *'Oh yes!'* But I was distinctly upset when she positively crooned over whatever John Bewley was doing with his new pen, on his new paper, to a wine bottle and a pile of courgettes that had never done him any harm.

I was delayed after the lesson, showing my portfolio to some of the experienced students. *'Oh, yes!'* they said. I left just behind Dorothea, herself closely following the dwarfish figure of poor John Bewley. I saw him get into her car. She had brought him, and was taking him home.

She brought him the following week. I sat in my car, and saw them arrive. Knowing where they both lived, I knew that she had come only a little out of her way. I was only a little more out of her way. He had her undivided attention, weekly, in the car both ways, as well as a grossly disproportionate share of her time during the class.

The thing was becoming seriously annoying.

John Bewley's manner in the class, at first so self-effacingly obsequious, became what I can only call 'cocky'. On arrival, he greeted and was greeted. Anything he had done, during the week, drew a crowd. He promoted himself from his ballpoint to a pen and Indian ink, and to brush and wash. I avoided looking at his drawings, when I could, out of pity, but I was obliged to glance at some of them.

'Oh, yes,' said Dorothea, looking at my pencil-poem of a coffee-pot. 'You ought to see what Mr Bewley has made of the same subject.'

I had to look. I had to grant that it was flashily effective, but I saw that there were blobs and blots. I had to make noises of agreement, even of admiration. I had, so to speak, to be a member of the club. John Bewley's exhibition of false modesty would have sickened a saint. I thanked God, in all humility, that I could still find the whole thing funny.

As my portfolio grew, so did my need – for which I think I may be forgiven – for recognition. I laboured early and late, at the classes and nearly every day between classes, playing upon pencil and paper as upon a sublime instrument of music. My range widened. I drew the garden from my windows; I derived audacious compositions from reproductions of the Old Masters; I thought about mounting and framing the best of them (some fifty drawings) and about an exhibition in the village hall.

But Dorothea Calloway was by some magic blinded. It was as though she had fallen under an unaccountable spell. I was legitimately disgruntled, but she was the real victim. Her judgement had been perverted, her priorities upturned, her profession betrayed, her taste diseased, all by the 'crush' that she had on John Bewley.

I did not hear, in the class, any comment about this unseemly situation. It was, of course, too obvious to require comment, too distasteful to permit it.

Occasionally Dorothea found a moment to make some comment on my drawings. I did not pay serious attention to what she said, in her present condition; I prayed only that she would 'snap out of it'.

Christmas approached, a break until the class reassembled in January. I was aghast. Angered and sickened as I was, I knew that I would miss the class dreadfully.

Perhaps the cold weather would carry off John Bewley. That would be the salvation of Dorothea, and her liberation; it would give her back eyes to see what I weekly laid before her.

We clubbed together to buy Dorothea a bottle of brown sherry for Christmas.

I had one of my drawings – a view of the garden from my window – mounted and glazed and framed, at considerable expense. I gave it to my niece and her husband for Christmas.

'Wherever shall we hang it?' cried she on Christmas morning.

'We'll have to think about that,' he said.

They hung it, I supposed, in their bedroom.

Somebody had given John Bewley for Christmas many tubes of 'Artist's' watercolour paint, a little metal palette, and a selection of brushes.

'Goody,' cried Dorothea Calloway, when he had unpacked his new toys. 'Let's have something *lurid*.'

His pad on his knee, he addressed himself to a 'set-up' of bright ceramic objects. I found the subject too crowded and fussy, and drew instead the delicate ruffles on a cabbage from Dorothea's garden.

She never even looked at it.

'You've been practising with these,' she said, looking over John Bewley's shoulder.

'No. First bash. Didn't know what to expect.'

'Piperesque,' said another pupil. 'Wonderfully dramatic.'

'I like bright colours,' said John Bewley, as though in apology, lapping up the praise of the class, which was given in imitation of Dorothea. More tastes were perverted, more judgements distorted, than Dorothea's only. John Bewley was a calamity to the lot of them.

'So do I,' said Dorothea; meaning, I suppose, that she also liked bright colours.

I knew that the gentle subtleties of my pencil, like Constable's, were more interesting, more artistic far, than the poster-like garishness of Bewley's painting. I had to clamp my jaw to stop myself saying so.

'Oh, here's Mr Love,' said Dorothea. 'I assume you'll do the teapot.'

I knew that one should expect the occasional failure. Perhaps I had a touch of influenza. Neither spout nor handle could be persuaded to go right.

'Yes,' said Dorothea, to whom I had not wished to show the drawing. 'Perhaps if you *looked harder* . . .'

A moment later she was deep in talk with John Bewley, with whom she had already spoken for ten minutes in her car. I heard him promise to try a drawing done first with the brush and afterwards with the pen.

He also, during the course of the spring, acquired charcoal, conté crayons, and sepia ink. With the last he drew not only with a pen but also with a matchstick stuck into a penholder, and a piece of sharpened bamboo. He was simply showing off.

'Nobody knows what John will do next,' said the class.

At the beginning of the 'Easter holidays' I repaired to the big stationer's in Mitchington, where, in a corner, they sold 'artist's materials'. I purchased nibs, and black and brown ink. Assiduously, all April, I practised the use of the pen. I purchased a fat brush and a thin one, and a bottle of soluble 'calligraphic' ink, and experimented with 'wash'.

They would see that John Bewley was not the only one who could branch adventurously out, who could astonish them, who could compel attention and admiration.

My niece was afraid I would spill Indian ink on my carpet, which was her carpet. The only time I did so, the stain was rather pleasing than otherwise. I nevertheless moved the coffee-table to cover it. Mrs Mallow, at her weekly 'Hoovering', discovered and reported it. I was crestfallen but no whit deterred. The quality that had been missing from my work was *dash*. I found that it was easy to drag an inadvertent cuff through wet ink, and trying to the patience to wait until it had dried.

With an air of fine unconcern I produced pen, nibs, brushes and inks at the very first class of the summer term.

Dorothea raised her eyebrows when she saw these things. I smiled, I think enigmatically; I said nothing; I set to work on a *strong and startling* drawing of a kettle.

Waiting for my ink to dry, I saw that John Bewley had acquired an easel. On it he had an oblong of hardboard, the shiny side of which he had (he said) primed with emulsion paint. I thought, for a moment of derisive astonishment, that he had embarked on oils, but I saw from his tubes of paint that he was working in acrylic.

He had evidently been practising. Perhaps he had had private lessons from Dorothea. He was doing it to draw attention to himself.

I went back to my ink, and to the first and palest wash.

'I do think,' said Dorothea, 'that you might be best to learn to walk before you try to run.'

Although she happened to be looking in my direction, I knew, of course, that her words were addressed to John Bewley.

I did drawings in faint pencil, thereafter, which I could rub out if things went wrong; only then did I allow myself the irremovable commitment of ink. I compared this realistic humility with the arrogant hubris of John Bewley.

I made a curious discovery, in the course of this

preliminary pencil work – pencil, faintly drawn, becomes invisible in strong direct light, but reappears when the pad is tilted into shadow. I have never heard or read of this phenomenon; I count it a genuine discovery.

As May passed into June, Dorothea had us out into the fields and spinneys, with old cottages, wooded hillsides, bridges over the canal for our subjects. We would reassemble at the end of the morning, Dorothea collecting John Bewley.

'Just *look* at Mr Bewley's picture,' cried Dorothea to the world at large. 'He's taken to landscape like a duck to water.'

I thought he had taken to landscape like a duck to land, all awkward, self-important, waddling clumsiness. It would have sounded like 'sour grapes' if I had said so. It was not that I grudged the old thing his harmless fun. It was the *wrongness* of Dorothea's opinion, the *credulity* of the class that echoed her, the *deplorable influence* it was having on the work of all the others, much of which *had been quite promising*. Isabel Craker was a prime example, most obvious to me since she and I, with John Bewley himself, were of the same first-year 'generation'. She might have developed the genuine, minor talent which I saw almost from the beginning. By following John Bewley's self-indulgent and self-advertising example, by being misled by Dorothea, herself misled, by joining the chorus of uncritical admiration of John Bewley, she had taken artistic turnings so fundamentally wrong that only by starting all over again could she redeem herself.

By the time of the summer 'half-term', it was clear to me that I was the only sane, objectively critical intelligence left in the Infants' School.

I cared passionately because, by now, art was the very

centre of my life. A day without a drawing was unthinkable. I needed, and bought, more portfolios, more and more pads. And the class had been, was still potentially, *so delightful and so excellent*. That Tuesday morning, with no class to go to, I thought about the class: and I heard a call as clear and peremptory as a church-bell in mid-winter. I was staggered by the revelation. The problem would not go away on its own, but *I could make it go away*. I gave the rest of the day, and much of the night, to making a plan.

I put it into operation immediately.

I knew that Tackham church was a celebrated subject for artists, viewed from the road on the other side of the valley. This was a private road, single-track, on land belonging to the Ministry of Defence. It had been made during the war, and unconvincingly maintained. It led only to what had then been an ammunition dump in Tackham Park. The ammunition had been, in large part, removed, so that the road led nowhere; although it was open to the public it was practically unused. Every few hundred yards there was a 'passing-place', as on minor roads in the Scottish Highlands. Such places doubled as lay-bys, for motorists who wished for any reason to stop, but were as infrequently used for this as for their original purpose. From one of the lay-bys the church could be most elegantly seen. There was room in the lay-by for a single car; another, parked for more than a moment, would have caused a dangerous obstruction.

On Wednesday morning I went there in my car, saying that I was going elsewhere, making the small necessary detour. I took my Polaroid camera. I stopped the car in the lay-by, and photographed the valley, the church picturesquely visible between trees. It was a truly enchanting scene, essence of the English countryside at once civilised and unspoiled; a modernist might have considered it, artistically, as something of a visual cliché. That would not deter John Bewley, whose daubs would escape glibness by dint of sheer incompetence.

From my photograph, and over the two full days of Thursday and Friday, I executed an intricate and fully-detailed pencil drawing of the scene, using the first page of a brand-new watercolour book. My pencil was faint. In direct lamplight or sunlight it was well-nigh invisible. From a few feet away, in full daylight, it *was* invisible. In shadow it was visible enough, so that it put me in mind of the ink used by a spy, which leaps into legibility only after the application of the proper chemical.

All Saturday, and Sunday afternoon, I practised drawing church and trees with my pen. I used inferior paper, and meticulously burned the results in my niece's incinerator. On Sunday morning I performed a duty equally necessary. I prayed for at least one fine Tuesday during the remaining four weeks of the term, and for John Bewley (and Dorothea) to agree to my suggestion.

On Monday I reconnoitred. I required a place where the body could be deposited so that it was discovered not immediately but soon, so that there should be no doubt about the time of death, and which was not less than forty and not more than forty-five mintues' drive from the roadside opposite Tackham church. My motoring map narrowed the possibilities. Main roads were to be used, for the anonymity of my vehicle and for a reliable mileage per hour; but the place had to be unobserved when I used it, but certain to be visited before, perhaps, one o'clock. The very place I wanted was the first I inspected, thanks to fruitful scrutiny of the map. I drove from there to the Tackham roadside in forty-two minutes. I filled the car with petrol, at a garage unknown to me, paying in cash. I bought a large spanner, one of a dozen in polythene bags on a spike in the garage office. There were motoring gloves in the car.

The moment I got home I put an empty cabin-trunk in the back seat of the car. It was not a thing my niece or her husband would notice. I could thus give a lift to one passenger, but only one.

Tuesday was the first of the last four art classes of the academic year. Each blank Tuesday, when the conjunction of circumstances was not right, perilously reduced the margin of error. But that Tuesday was blank, because we all went to a lock on the canal, and some painted the reflections in the water, some the lock-keeper's cottage, and John Bewley what Dorothea absurdly called a 'space-age Ivor Hitchens'.

The following Tuesday it rained, and we sat in front of bowls of midsummer flowers. Dorothea said John Bewley's flower picture was 'by Matisse out of Fantin-Latour', which was the greatest rubbish I ever heard. Of my pen-and-wash drawing over traces of pencil she had nothing to say at all.

Half the possible days had gone. Two only remained. I forced myself to continue to practise drawing in ink with an untrembling hand.

The third of those Tuesdays, the penultimate class until September. I was up with the misty dawn, looking anxiously at the sky. Conditions promised a 'scorcher'. I checked and double-checked my equipment. Gloves and untouched spanner in the car. Pencil, India rubber, penholder, nibs, two brushes, Indian and calligraphic inks, a flask of water, a flat glass dish, a knife. The new watercolour book with the pencil drawing of the church, two days' work, on the first of its virgin pages. I needed nothing else and I took nothing else.

I spilled my breakfast coffee. I took a drastic grip of myself. Everything I had learned of self-discipline would be needed this golden day.

Human awkwardness, perversity, selfishness were all that I had to fear.

I arrived at the Infants' School five mintues early. Other cars began to arrive. The pupils chatted in the car-park, enjoying the sunshine, enjoying the prospect of *plein-air* painting. Dorothea arrived, with John Bewley crouched like a ferret beside her. I was at his window even as Dorothea pulled up her handbrake, holding my new watercolour pad.

I said, 'If ever there was a day for Tackham church . . .'

Bewley seemed to demur. I could not press too hard. The whole scheme hung poised, waiting on the whim of one silly and spoiled old man.

Ironically, Dorothea decided him. 'Bully idea!' she said. 'Only room for one car, if you mean the place I think you mean.'

'No problem,' I said. 'My car holds two.'

'Ah, would you very kindly . . .?' said John Bewley. 'I'll hoist my clobber out of the back of this one.'

'I'll come for you about twelve-thirty,' said Dorothea, 'in case Mr Love wants to go straight home. I doubt if I'll make it before.'

'I thought we might start at once,' I said.

'Spot on,' said John Bewley. 'Have as long as possible with the church.'

'*Etonnez-moi*,' said Dorothea.

John Bewley simpered, and transferred his equipment from her car to mine.

105

'Brand-new book,' I said to Dorothea, riffling the pages to show her that they were all blankly white. That very first page, in the strong sunlight, was, from where she was sitting, blankly white.

'Christen it with a goody,' she said.

Old Major Patterson wanted to come to Tackham church too. I showed him the trunk in the back of my car, and reminded him about the little lay-by. There was an ugly moment when Patterson seemed to be beseeching, and John Bewley to be about to yield him the place in my car. But all his equipment – easel, paints, palette, brushes – was now stacked on the trunk in the car, and Patterson faced the fact that he had, in an almost literal sense, missed the bus.

John Bewley and I arrived at the lay-by at 10.31.

He set up his easel, and immediately began working. At least he had energy – he went at that painting 'bald-headed'. I strolled away, and sat on the wall beside the road. I was no more than a dozen yards from John Bewley, but out of his sight because of the car. It was now 10.37. I felt suffocated with excitement. I willed my hand to obey me. I tilted my pad so that it was in shadow. Into faint visibility leaped my drawing of a month before, fourteen and more hours of painstaking work.

I inked in the drawing, working as fast as I dared, going from the top left-hand corner to the bottom right. It was not one of my very best, but it was not far from my best. I was interested that work under extreme pressure of time, and extreme emotional pressure, could be so lyrically and pastorally tranquil. I put down the pad in full sun, to dry the ink as fast as possible. It was now 10.47. While the ink dried, I strolled to John Bewley's position, as we were all wont to do. He seemed to be painting entirely in a sick yellow. I could not imagine what he was at. I returned to my pad, and poured a little water into the glass dish. With the larger of my brushes I added a dollop of calligraphic ink. I washed the brush, and started to lay in the wash – the sky, leaving white for the clouds; the shadows in the trees and those cast by the trees; the shaded aspects of the church. The paper was dripping wet. It was now 10.51. I hid the pad by the wall out of sight. I put pen, brushes and the rest beside it. I walked to the car. I was quite cool. I knew that the sound of an opening car door would distract John Bewley, if at all, for a moment only. He did not in fact look up from his work. He was adding areas of green to his yellow. He was making a mess. I put on the gloves. With my knife I slit open the polythene bag of the spanner. I moved softly from the car to a position a yard behind John Bewley.

A thousand things could still go wrong, at this phase and at every later phase.

John Bewley was splashing a blueish paint into his riot of green and yellow. I supposed that in his mind the landscape was taking shape. I would spare the world that.

His narrow freckled skull reflected the sunlight with as much brilliance as the windscreen of my car. It was cleaner than the windscreen.

I do not in my mind dwell on the next few seconds. I think I killed him outright with the spanner. Certainly he crumpled, without a sound. I caught him, avoiding blood, at the same time pulling his jacket over his head. I made sure he was dead by throttling him, listening all the time for the great improbability of traffic. I took his wallet from the breast pocket of his coat, and put it in my own. I put the spanner, unpleasantly spattered, into his trouser pocket. I wrapped the jacket tight round his head, tying the sleeves, so that nothing would drip in my car. I dragged him to the car and bundled him on to the floor behind the front seat. He was light. He fitted well, when doubled up. He was invisible, with the jacket over his head.

I checked my drawing. The wash was still wet. I admired the drawing, which looked better with the pale wash over much of it. I looked forward keenly to returning to it. As I slid under the wheel of the car, I glanced at John Bewley's 'painting' on the easel. I had decided to leave it there. It was now 10.56. I was astonished that my recent actions had taken only five minutes: it occurred to me that my watch had stopped, but the clock in the car confirmed the time.

I took off the gloves. I drove to Corsley, rapidly but taking no risks. One of the things that could go wrong was a breakdown, which would mean inevitable discovery of the body. A smash. A road under repair, blocked, diverted, a police patrol, census-takers, puncture . . . The most probable disaster was Dorothea's arrival at the lay-by before her time. It was long odds against. I had an explanation ready. My alibi remained valid. There were, oh there were, so many other improbable but possible hazards.

Nobody paid any attention to me on the road, although I felt as though a spotlight were following me, lurid as John Bewley's 'painting'. I arrived without hitch at Corsley at 11.40 precisely, having taken forty-four minutes. That was only two minutes outside my 'test-lap' time, and left a barely sufficient margin.

Corsley was a community on the edge of a considerable town; it had, on its own edge, a large Comprehensive School, set, together with a sports centre, in an area of scrubby pinewoods. There were always a lot of cars parked on its acres of tarmac. But at noon on a weekday there would be few people about, those avoidable. I parked. If there were people about I did not see them, or they me. I resumed the gloves. Under cover of a parked minibus, I bundled the body out of the car, into the edge of the scrub. I kept the jacket wrapped about the head, so that no blood escaped on to anything that was mine. The spanner fell out of the jacket pocket. I pitched it, still untouched by human finger since it was packaged in its place of manufacture, into the undergrowth. I took the money out of the wallet (why not? He had no use for it); I left the credit cards and so forth. I threw the wallet, untouched by my hands, into the brush. It would be found, with the spanner, probably not immediately, and the body thus identified. That was good.

I worked fast; the turn-round took only three minutes. I left the gigantic car-park, unnoticed as when I arrived, at 11.43. I drove back to Tackham. I disposed, on the way, of the gloves and the plastic envelope which had held the spanner. They simply joined piles of other rubbish. Their existence would not be suspected; they would not be found; if they were, they could not be traced to me.

I was less at risk on the way back, since the car was perfectly clean. But the dangers remained appalling. Cars were infrequent on the road across the valley from the church, but if one passed, stopped, the people stayed and stayed? If Dorothea changed her mind, and arrived at the lay-by at noon? John Bewley's easel, no sign of him, no sign of me, of my car. It was one of the risks that simply had to be taken.

My hands sweated as I drove. I went as fast as I dared. I could not think of anything I could do, anything I had not done, to improve the odds in my favour.

I turned the corner fifty yards from the lay-by. Nothing. Nobody. I began to dare to hope that it had worked. It was 12.24. I had cut it extremely fine. I hurried to my point of vantage, recovered my pad, mixed new and darker wash with the calligraphic ink.

I was adding the darker wash to the shadows within the trees of my drawing when Dorothea's car rumbled up.

'Great Scot,' she said, 'where's Mr Bewley?'

'Is he not there?' I said.

'When did you last see him?'

'It was – hum – I simply don't know. I've been working flat out.'

'I can see you have. Yes, there's a lot of work in that. Bully for you.'

Bully for me. Already things were changing.

The body was discovered, as I later learned, at almost exactly the moment I got back to Tackham. The police searched the surrounding scrubland, and found the wallet whose contents identified the body, and the spanner which was evidently the murder weapon.

Robbery was considered a possible motive; the victim was known, by his family, to have been carrying some money, intending to go shopping after the art lesson. But he still wore his watch, and his credit cards had not been taken. The oddity, of course, was the distance of the body from the place where he had last been seen.

There was no doubt that he had been there, even without my evidence. He was seen leaving the Infants' School in my car; he had left an unfinished painting at Tackham, evidently *of* Tackham, unmistakably his work.

Every common-sense argument pointed to me as the murderer. I had known that this would be so. But I had done an elaborate, detailed pencil drawing of that landscape (the pencil even now visible here and there under the ink) and though the pen-work and brush-work could have been done quite rapidly, 'even by me', the pencil drawing must have taken an hour – well over an hour. Dorothea told the police so. She had seen me working, learning, since the previous September. She knew exactly what I was capable of, the speed I was capable of. It was flatly impossible, indeed, that *anybody* – John Bewley, Dorothea herself – could have achieved what I had achieved in twenty minutes. And twenty minutes were all I could have taken for the drawing, if I had driven all the way to Corsley and back.

The police were unhappy that I could tell them nothing about other cars, people, John Bewley's disappearance on foot or by any other means. I told them, self-deprecating, that an artist hard at work was *blind to the world*. This was fortunately confirmed by Dorothea and her other pupils. As a breed we were, when the fit was upon us, *passionately single-minded*.

I was very nearly charged. A lifetime's experience had made me sensitive to unstated official attitudes. I was *very* nearly charged, because it was incredible to the Director of Public Prosecutions that a man could be murdered and removed (they knew, from traces of blood on the roadside, that he had been killed in front of his 'painting') without another man, a dozen yards away, in full possession of his faculties, being aware of the fact.

But when all was said, suspected, hinted, brooded upon, the bald certainty remained – I could not have produced the drawing I produced unless I had spent all morning at Tackham. It was an alibi unprecedented in the annals of the criminal law.

It was a gloomy occasion, that last class of the summer. There had been talk of cancelling it, but 'John would not have wanted that'. It rained. My pen-and-wash still life of aluminium kitchenware was, not unnaturally, lit by a curious radiance, emitting a convincing and magical metallic gleam.

'Much more like it,' said Dorothea, looking over my shoulder longer than she had *ever done before.*

It was with a buoyant heart that I contemplated a gloriously inky summer. For my birthday in July I asked only for 'artist's materials'.

I came on, all summer, by 'leaps and bounds'. When I was not doing my work, I was looking at it. Every piece was dated and, of course, signed.

I looked forward with passionate eagerness to the new season's art classes in September. What *would* they all say?

The great day. My armfuls of paraphernalia. The good wishes of my niece. Old faces and new ones.

We experienced 'old sweats' settled ourselves immediately in front of the various still-life arrangements Dorothea was setting up. We spared a tolerant glance at the 'new boys'. Six of them, four women; a normal proportion. One of the women was about my age, somewhat swarthy, white-haired, walking with a stick, her voice, heard to excess, a kind of sing-song. She would not become an irritant because she would not become an artist.

I worked with a confidence and certainty born of those hundreds of drawings I had done in the summer. No longer for me the hesitant pencil before the exclamatory ink. My biggest brush for the wash. A touch of crayon.

Dorothea's eye, as she tacked about the Infants' School, lit on my drawing. It seemed to rove away, having registered nothing.

112

She was looking now at the hands, heads, bowls, upturned stools of the beginners. She was positive, encouraging, to each. She came to the Indian lady, a Mrs da Silva.

'My God,' she said, 'I don't know who taught you, but they taught you more than I can.'

'Nobody. I come all ignorant to this.'

'Impossible.'

Isabel Craker, Major Patterson and the others agreed that it was impossible. I am thankful to have forgotten the saccharine adjectives which they used about Mrs da Silva's drawings.

'It's old John Bewley all over again.'

That it was.

The Pomeranian Poisoning

Peter Lovesey

Rosebud Books
Volumes of Romance
Battersea Bridge Road
London SW11
12th May

Dearest Honeypot,

Have you gone into hiding? My telephonist has a sore finger from trying your number, and your Grizzly Bear is going spare. Can't work, can't think of anything else. Horrid fears that his Honeypot has been stolen by some other bear and taken to another part of the forest.

Put him out of his misery, won't you, and tell him it isn't true? The weekend in Brighton wasn't so disappointing as all that, was it? The trouble with this bear is that he's too excitable when he gets the chance of Honey, but he remains huggingly affectionate. He passionately wants another chance to prove it.

Do pick up the blower and comfort your fretful

Grizzly

PS Are you writing anything at present? A brilliant opportunity has cropped up. Couldn't possibly make Honeypot any sweeter, but could guarantee to make her infinitely richer.

310 Arch Street

Earls Court

SW5

Sunday afternoon

Dear Frank (I'd rather drop the nursery names, if you don't mind),

As you see, I've moved from Fulham. Your letter was sent on. Take a deep breath and pour yourself a double scotch, Frank. I'm living with a guy called Tristram. He's my age and could pass for my twin brother and we have so much in common that I can hardly believe it's true. We both adore Status Quo, Martin Amis, Chinese takeaways, Steve Bell, Porsches, Spielberg, Daley Thompson, goose-down duvets and so much else it would take the rest of today and next week to list it. Tristram went to public school (Radley) and Sussex University. He had a degree in American Studies and he's terribly high-powered. He knows Milton Friedman and James Baldwin and masses of people who come up on the box. I know you'll understand when I say that I'm totally committed to Tristram now.

Pause, for you to top up the scotch.

Frank, I want you to know that this has nothing to do with what happened, or didn't quite happen, that Saturday night in Brighton. I blame that bottle of Asti. We should have stayed on g. and t. Whatever, no hard feelings, OK?

I'm not sure if you still feel the same about the business

opportunity you mentioned, but I *am* quite intrigued, as a matter of fact. Yes, I've been doing some writing – tinkering away at a novel about the women's movement, the first of a five-book saga, actually – but Tristram and I are both on social security so I wouldn't mind putting the novel on one side if there's cash on tap now. But I must make it clear that it's my writing talent, such as it is, that's up for grabs, and nothing else. Putting it another way, Frank darling, I'm open to advances in pounds sterling.

We don't have a phone yet, and it gets expensive using pay-phones, so be a darling and write by return.

> Be kind to me.
>
> Luv,
>
> Felicity

Rosebud Books
Volumes of Romance

23 May

Dear Felicity,

You may wonder why it took me so long to answer your letter; on the other hand, you may wonder that I bothered to answer it at all. I need hardly say that I am deeply hurt. For me, the age difference between us was never an impediment, and I rashly imagined you felt the same way. You gave me no reason to suppose there was anyone else in your life. You appeared to enjoy our evenings together. True, I caught you closing your eyes at the proms from time to time, but I took it that you were transported by the music. You always seemed to revive in time for our suppers in the trattoria. I find myself putting a cynical construction on everything now.

I suppose I must accept that I was just a meal-ticket, or a sugar-daddy, or whatever cruel phrase is currently in vogue for it.

As to that literary project I happened to mention, I shall obviously look elsewhere. The work required is undemanding and I dare say I shall have no difficulty finding an author willing to make a six-figure sum for a short children's book.

You may keep my LP of the Enigma Variations. To listen to it ever again would be too distressful.

Your former friend,

Franklin.

310 Arch Street,
SW5
Wednesday morning

Grizzly Darling!

What a wild, ferocious bear you were last night! Honeypot has never felt so stirred.

When I arrived with the Elgar and the Mateus Rosé, I honestly meant to say sorry and a civilised goodbye. You're so masterful!

If you still mean what you said (and if you don't I shall throw myself under a train) could you come with the van some time between six-thirty and seven on Friday evening? Tristram will be at his Karate class and it will avoid a scene that might otherwise be too hairy for us all. I haven't much stuff to move out, darling. One trip will be enough, I'm sure.

Hugs and kisses,

Your

Felicity

My own dearest Tristram,

Please, darling, before you do anything else, read this to the end. It's terribly important to our relationship that you understand what I have done, and why.

I've moved out. I'm going to stay with Frank, that doddery old publisher guy I told you about. Before you blow your top, Tris, hear me out. I've agonised over this for days. Darling, you know I wouldn't walk out on you without a copper-bottomed reason. Frank means nothing to me. He's a dingbat: pathetic, ugly, flabby, but – and this is the point – he knows a way to make me fabulously rich. I mean stinking rich, Tris. We're talking telephone numbers. And for what? For some book he wants me to write. He hasn't given me all the details yet. He's boxing clever until I move in with him, which is part of the deal, but I understand it's only a children's book he wants. I can finish it in a matter of days if I pull out all the stops, and then I'll be off like a bunny, sweetheart.

He insisted that I go and live in his house in the backwoods of Surrey while I'm writing the thing. Isn't it a bore? I'm not giving you the address because I know what you'll do. You'll be down there kicking in the door, and who could blame you? But just pause to think.

If I pass up this opportunity, what sort of future do you and I have? I mean, I *know* it's terrific being together, but what prospect is there of ever getting out of this damp slum? I've had enough, Tris, and so have you. Admit it.

I can almost hear you say I'm selling myself, and I suppose I am if I'm honest, but, let's face it, I spent a weekend with Frank in Brighton before I met you. It's not as if he's a total stranger. And if I am selling myself, what a price!

Which is why I'm asking you to keep your cool and try to understand that this is the best chance we've got. Just a short interval, darling, and then we can really start to live.

There won't be a minute when you're out of my thoughts, lover.

I'll write again soon.
Be patient, darling!
Ever your

Felicity

This dreary pad in Surrey
Saturday night

Dearest Tristram,

Has it been only a week? It feels like *months*. A life sentence with hard labour, and I've been doing plenty of that. Writing, I mean. Non-stop. The reason I can do so much is that I know every word, every letter, I write is worth pounds and pounds. Guaranteed. It's crazy, but it's true. I'm on to a winner, Tris. You see, Frank – he's my publisher-friend – has told me exactly how this is going to work, and he's right. It can't miss. He and I are going to split – wait for it – half a million dollars!

For a kids' book?

Yes!

Scrape yourself off the floor and I'll tell you how this miracle works.

You know that Frank is the chairman of Rosebud Books, who publish romance fiction, and before you knock it, remember that my only published work, *Desire Me Do*, paid for our new telly, among other things. Frank's outfit isn't exactly Mills & Boon, but he helps beginners like me to get started and I dare say it makes life more tolerable for a few thousand readers of the things.

One of Frank's regular writers was an eccentric old biddy called Zenobia Hatt. That was her real name, believe it or not. I'm using the past tense because she died four or five years ago, before I got to know Frank. Apparently she was prolific. Her books didn't sell all that well, but she kept producing them. And she expected to see them in the shops. Every time she walked into a supermarket and spotted a display of paperbacks, she checked to see if her latest was among them. If it wasn't, she made a beeline for Rosebud Books to tear a strip off Frank. She was always tearing strips off Frank. Even if the book was in the shop, something about it would upset her, like the cover design, or the quality of paper they were using. I don't know why he continued to publish her, but he did. She always appeared with her two dogs in tow. They were Pomeranians. If you think I'm rabbiting on about nothing important, you're making a big mistake. This *is* important.

Do you know about Pomeranians? They're toy dogs. Funny little beggars with enormous ruffs, neat faces and tiny legs. They come in most colours. You know how some old ladies are with dogs? Zenobia doted on hers.

Well, like I said, she died, and this is the important bit, Tristy. In her will, she left the house and everything she had to be divided between her relatives. That is, except any future income from her books. You get royalties trickling in long after a book is published, you see. Zenobia decreed that the future profits from her writing should go into a trust fund to pay for her dogs to be kept in style in some rip-off place in Hampstead that caters for pampered pets who have come into money. The residue was to be awarded annually as a literary prize: the Zenobia Hatt prize.

Nice idea, right? The snag was that Zenobia wasn't

really in the Barbara Cartland class as a best-selling writer. The royalties paid the fees at the dogs' home for a couple of years and then the Pommies were put down. There was never any residue, so the prize was never awarded.

End of story? Not quite. Cop this, love.

A couple of months ago, Frank had a phone call from California. Some film producer was asking about the rights to a Rosebud book called *Michaela and the Mount*, by – you guessed – Zenobia Hatt! It was a cheap romance she published years ago, so long ago, in fact, that it was out of print, so Frank wouldn't make a penny out of any deal. Don't ask me why, but this book is reckoned to be the perfect vehicle for some busty starlet they reckon is the next Madonna.

Tris, darling, they bought it for half a million bucks! The money goes into the trust and by the terms of Zenobia's will it has to be offered as the prize for 1987. The lot. The doggies aren't on the payroll any more, so every silver dollar is up for grabs. And who do you think is going to win?

Shall I tell you how? The point is that Zenobia didn't offer her money for any common or garden novel. She had very clear ideas about the sort of book she wanted to encourage. She had it written into her will that the prize should go to the best published work of fiction that featured a Pomeranian dog as one of the main characters. As you can imagine, that limits the competition somewhat.

When Frank cottoned on to this, he did some quick thinking. Animal stories don't usually feature on the Rosebud list, but he reckoned he could stretch a point and commission a book for kids featuring Tom the Pom that he'd rush through before the end of the year to scoop the prize. He'd go fifty-fifty with the writer, and that's me, sweetheart. I've signed an agreement and pay-day will be some time in January, when the trustees award the prize. It's as simple as that. No one else has time to get a book out, because the news hasn't broken yet, and won't until the film deal is finalised. You know what American lawyers are like. Well, perhaps you don't, but the trustees expect to sign the contract in October or November. *Tom the Pom* will hit the shops in time for Christmas and it doesn't matter a brass farthing how many it sells, because it's certain to clean up half a million bucks.

That's the story so far, my love. Naturally I can't wait to finish *my* story and hand it over. Then there'll be nothing to keep me here. I hope to see you Friday at the latest, and what a reunion that will be . . .

Luv you,

Felicity

Same Place, Unfortunately
Thursday

Tris, darling,

I'm not going to make it by tomorrow. I showed Frank what I've written so far and he wants some changes, some of them pretty drastic. I tried pointing out that it didn't really matter if the writing was sloppy in places, so long as I finished the flaming book and it got into print before the end of the year, but he came over all high and mighty and sounded off about standards and the reputation of his house. I wondered what on earth his house had to do with it until I discovered he was talking about Rosebud Books, his publishing house. He says he doesn't want an inferior book to carry his imprint, especially as *Tom the Pom* is certain to get a lot of attention when it wins. I suppose he has a point.

So it's back to the keyboard to hammer out some revisions. What a drag!

I suppose Monday or Tuesday would be a realistic estimate.

Impatiently,

Luv,

Felicity

Wednesday

Oh, Tris,

I'm so depressed! I've had the mother and father of a row with Frank. I finished the book yesterday, with all the changes he wanted. He read it last night. He wasn't exactly over the moon, but he agreed it couldn't wait any longer, so he would hand it over to his sub-editor. I said fine, and would he kindly drop me and my baggage at the flat on his way to the office. Tris, he looked at me as if I was crazy. He said we had an agreement. I said certainly we had, and I'd fulfilled my side of it by finishing the book. Now I was ready to go home.

Whereupon he deluged me with a load of gush about how it was much more than a publishing agreement to him. He wouldn't have asked me to write the book if he hadn't believed I was willing to move in with him. I meant more to him than all the money and if I walked out on him now he would drop the typescript in the Thames.

Tris, I'm sure he means it. He knows I need the money and he's going to keep me here like a hostage until the book is in the shops. He could cancel it at any stage up to then. I'll be here for *months*.

There's no way out that I can see. You and I are just going to have to be patient. The day the book is published, I'll be free. And ready to collect my share of the prize. Let's go ski-ing in February, shall we? And what sort of car shall we buy? We can have that Porsche. One each, if we want. If we both look forward to next year, perhaps we can get through. We *must* get through.

Tris, don't try and trace me here, darling. It would be too painful for us both.

I'm thinking of you constantly.

Your soon-to-be-rich, but sorry-to-be-here

Felicity

As Before
1 August.

Tris, my love,

Did you wonder if I was ever going to write again? Are you starting to doubt my existence? Dear God, I hope not. The reason it has been so long is that I get dreadfully depressed. I've written any number of letters and destroyed them when I read them through a second time. It's no good for me to wallow in self-pity, and it certainly won't do much for you.

So this time, I'll be positive. Another month begins today. For me, another milestone. I've endured ten weeks now, and I'm still looking at my watch all day long.

I expect you'd like to know how I pass my days. I get up around nine, after he's left for work. Breakfast (half a grapefruit, coffee and toast), then a walk if it's fine. Without giving anything away – and I won't, so don't look for clues – there are some beautiful walks through the woods here. I see squirrels every day and sometimes deer. Often I collect enough mushrooms to have on toast for lunch, or if I'm really energetic I might put them into a quiche. The rest of the morning and most of the afternoon is devoted to my writing. The novel, I mean. It's slow work, but it's good stuff, Tris, a sight better than *Tom the Pom*, which is going to make so much more money. Crazy. (*T. the P.* was in proof four weeks ago, by the way, and this is the good news: LIBERATION DAY is earlier than I dared to hope – September 30th.) Later in the afternoon I might do some reading. The trouble is that the only books here are Rosebud Romances, which depress me, even if they're sufficiently well written to be readable, and boring non-fiction on hunting, shooting and fishing that he only keeps for the leather bindings.

Around six I get something out of the freezer for the evening meal. He comes down about seven and that's all I'm going to say about my day. I stop living then.

Perhaps you wonder why I don't slip away to London during the day to see you. Tris, I've often thought of it. I know that I couldn't bear to come back here if I did. He'd stop publication of the book and you and I would have endured all this for nothing. No, I must hold out here.

Less than two months to go!

Love,

Felicity

The Same
19th August

Tris darling,

I have a horrid feeling that Frank suspects something. It's like this. Ever since he moved me here, he's assumed that it's for keeps. He constantly talks about his future as if I'm part of it. Like he talks about the two of us (him and me) taking trips on Concorde or the Orient Express when we've got our hands on the Zenobia Hatt prize. Naturally

I go along with this, letting him think I can't imagine anything more blissful than sharing the rest of my life with him and half a million bucks.

Up to now, I'm sure he's believed me. Up to last night, anyway. Then, out of the blue, he mentioned you, Tris. I don't think either of us have spoken your name since he brought me here. He asked me if I'd been in touch with you, and of course I denied it. Just to sound more convincing, I went a bit further and said I'd forgotten all about you.

Frank went on to say that he only happened to speak of you because by chance he was driving along Arch Street at lunchtime yesterday and he saw a tall, dark guy in leathers coming out of number 310 with his arm around a strikingly good-looking redhead. I must admit he caught me off guard for a moment. I must have looked concerned, because he took me up on it at once and asked why I'd gone so pale.

I see now that it was a shabby, underhand trick to test my reactions. I can't fathom how he knows that you go in for leathers, because I've never told him, but I'm sure of one thing, and that's that you wouldn't cheat on me while I'm in purgatory here.

If Frank wants a battle of wits, he'll find I'm more than a match for him. I think last night was just a try-on, but I'm taking no chances. I'll make sure no one sees me posting this.

I've discovered a way of making my walks more interesting. Among those boring old books on blood sports in the library I found an illustrated guide on the fungi of Great Britain. I take it with me and try and identify the different species along the paths. I'm doing quite well so far, with four different sorts of toadstools as well as the mushrooms I have for lunch.

127

Six weeks today and we'll be together, Tris. For keeps.
I'll write when I can.
Miss you so much.

Felicity

Still Holed-Up Here
September 10th

Well, Tris, my darling,

It's a day for celebration. I've actually had a copy of *Tom the Pom* in my hands! The printers have delivered it on time. But before you uncork the champagne, let me explain that this still isn't publication day. That remains the same, September 30th. They send the books out to the shops ready for the big day, but no one is supposed to sell them before then. In theory, Frank could cancel the publication, call them back and burn them all, and I actually believe he would if he knew I was planning to give him the elbow once I've qualified for the prize.

The book strikes me as pretty abysmal now that I've had a chance to read it again. However, they've dressed it up in a shiny laminated cover with cute illustrations by some artist (who won't have any claim on the prize, incidentally, because it's awarded to the writer) and I expect they'll sell a few hundred.

I'm glad to have something to give me a boost, because Frank has been driving me mad. He keeps wanting assurances that I'm committed to him for life, and he constantly paws me. I think he senses that I find it disagreeable, and that makes him even more persistent. He often mentions you now, and that redhead he is supposed to have seen you with. It's as if he senses what's in my mind and wants me to break down and admit it.

Sometimes I feel so angry that I'd like to stop him getting *any* of the prize, like the poms that were put down before they could come into a fortune. You and I would be twice as well off then.

I do my best to divert myself on my walks, which I'm now taking morning and afternoon, in all weathers. I'm becoming quite an expert on fungi. I've found and identified several more species, including *Amanita Phalloides*, known commonly as the Death Cap or the Destroying Angel. Not to be confused with the mushroom, as it is fatal if eaten. There's a small crop of them under an oak only five minutes from here.

Only three weeks now, my love!

Felicity

Here, but not for much longer
One day to Liberation!

Darling Tristram,

By the time you get this, it will be Publication Day and I will have freed myself from Frank for ever. He has become quite insufferable.

I've come to a momentous decision. It's been forced on me partly because I'm desperately frightened to tell him that I'm leaving him. I don't want the confrontation, and I know that if I just walk out, he'll track me down. I don't ever want to see him again. He gives me the creeps. And I feel bitter that he's due to collect such a large share of the prize. It's supposed to go to the writer, Tris, and I was the one who slogged it out for days inventing a story. Frank didn't do a damn thing except hand it to the printer.

I want you to do something for me, Tris. Please,

darling, burn every one of the letters I wrote you. I don't want anyone to know I was ever here. *Make sure you do this.*

Trust me, whatever happens, because I love you.

Felicity

6.30

Dear Grizzly,

Quiche in the oven.

Honeypot

Sydney, Australia
25th April

Dear Felicity,

I'm not sure whether you're permitted to receive letters in prison, particularly letters from former boyfriends. Maybe you don't want to hear from me anyway, but I think I owe you some kind of explanation. If it upsets you, well, you've got thirty years to get over it.

I followed your trial in the Aussie papers. They covered it quite fully in the tabloids. Apparently murder by poisoning is still a good paper-seller. They don't have death-cap toadstools here, but there are other kinds of poisonous fungi that I suppose one could disguise in a quiche. The reports I read suggested that you didn't know it would take up to a week for Frank to die. Books on fungi don't always go into that sort of detail. I wondered why they couldn't save him by washing out his stomach or something, but apparently the toxins are absorbed before the first effects appear. Looking at it from his point of view, at least he lived long enough to tell his suspicions to the police.

You'll notice I haven't given an address above. That

isn't from secrecy. It's because I'm on a cruise around the world. Some months ago I met this gorgeous redhead called Imogen. To be brutally honest, she moved in with me at Earls Court after you went to live with Frank. I got lonely, Fel, and I figured you had company, so why shouldn't I?

Imogen is one of those quiet girls who are capable of surprising you. I didn't know she found a bunch of your letters to me and secretly read them. I didn't know she had any talent as a children's writer until last January, when she was announced as the winner of the Zenobia Hatt prize. I don't suppose you had a chance to see the press reports. The trustees received only two entries. Imogen's *One Hundred and Two Pomeranians*, which she published privately at her own expense in December, was adjudged to be closest to the spirit of the award.

No hard feelings? The cash wouldn't have been much use to you, would it?

Cheers, love.

Tristram

A Good Wife

Dyan Sheldon

Reverend Ram's sermon for Mother's Day was: 'Is Motherhood Old-fashioned?' As soon as he announced it, leaning over the pulpit like it was a question he really expected to have answered, there was a flutter of movement among the young people and the men all settled back for a rest. Lettie Brahms, who was sitting next to me as usual, looked at her watch. What the Reverend Ram eventually decided was that, no, motherhood is not old-fashioned or obsolete, that being a wife and homemaker is even more important than it ever was before. 'I'm sure glad to hear that,' Lettie whispered. 'I wouldn't want to go to my grave thinking I'd wasted most of my life.'

It was a warm, sunny day, almost lazy with springtime. Even though the doors were shut you could smell the new leaves and the lilacs in the garden next door. I've always thought that being in church is like being suspended in time. Sometimes, sitting there, I forget what year it is, what's happening outside, what's waiting for me when the sermon's over and I've gone back home.

One Sunday morning could be any other; it might be Lettie beside me or someone else – my mother, my sister, one of my own kids, young and twitchy and more interested in what was for dinner than what the minister has to say, or James, listening to the scripture with that solemn expression on his face, as though he was checking that God hadn't gotten anything wrong. And that's how I felt on Mother's Day morning, while the heads in front of me nodded every so often and Dr Ram explained about the Christian marriage, and Mr Weimer, the usher, coughed discreetly at the back of the church – I felt like it was another time, a different congregation, a younger me. As though it's that easy to get back to the past – get back and hold on.

'You girls just on the brink of womanhood, you young wives just settling down into your lives – I want you to ask yourselves this: What is a good wife? I want you to say to yourselves: How can I be a good wife? How can I be a good mother? I want you to search your hearts and minds and ask yourselves: Do I know what God really wants of me? Do I know what is really important to Him?' The men all seemed to raise their chins a little, confident that they knew the answers.

'He can talk himself blue in the face,' Lettie was saying as we stepped out into the sunshine, 'but the plain fact is that things have changed.'

There was a young woman pushing one of those stroller things down the street. She had light blonde hair, and she was talking away to the baby even though she was walking like she was in a hurry.

'It's not the same as when we were young, Louise. Everything's different now. Upside down. These girls today don't know what their duty is, let alone how to do it. They're just out for themselves.'

134

I suppose it was the combination of that pale hair, just sort of pinned up on her head to get it out of the way, and Reverend Ram's sermon, but I was suddenly reminded of Ann Carlson so strongly that I nearly cried out.

'Look at that girl,' I said, grabbing Lettie by the arm and jerking her around. 'Doesn't she remind you of Ann?'

Lettie squinted down the street. 'That's the one moved into the Lustigs' old house. Her husband's some sort of engineer. Sally Beth says he used to work down at Cape Canaveral.'

It's never been easy to keep Lettie to the point. 'But don't you think she looks like Ann?' I repeated. 'Doesn't she remind you of Ann?'

Lettie resettled her white straw bag on her arm and grabbed hold of the rail as we walked down the stairs. 'Ann who?'

'Carlson,' I said, about ready to shake her. 'Ann Carlson. Don't you remember her? Her husband ran away with another woman right before Christmas. Must've been nineteen-fifty or fifty-one.'

'Was that the year we were snowed in most of the winter? The time they set up a food depot in the fire station and Leroy Kennedy skied across the bay?'

'Yes,' I said. 'That was the year.'

Lettie shook her head. 'I don't remember her at all. I remember him. George. He was always one for the ladies, wasn't he, George? Always a bit wild. Too handsome, I always thought. You couldn't forget him.'

But it's Ann I can't forget.

In the forty years that have passed since that winter I don't think so much as one week has passed that I haven't thought about Ann – wondered about her, remembered. George Carlson's face (a face I grew up with, a face once as familiar to me as my own) is just a memory, an image at the back of my mind, but Ann's is so vivid it seems almost real. I can still see her exactly as he was the first time we met. And I can still see her as she was that last time, smiling at me and James as she backed the car out of the driveway, thanking us for everything, promising to write. She had her hair up, making her look older, more tired. I stooped down by the window to say one last goodbye, and for a second she hesitated, looking right into my eyes as though she was going to say something or was waiting for me to say something. And then James bent down beside me, giving her some last-minute advice about her route, and she said, 'I'll write you as soon as I get there.' But of course she never did. Years after she and the baby'd gone back to Illinois – after their house had been repainted and modernised and had changed hands several times, after the women at the church had stopped talking about George and all the things he was meant to have done and about Ann and how much she'd suffered – years later James would sometimes say, 'I wonder what ever happened to that poor woman, what was her name . . . George Carlson's wife. Remember her? I always felt sorry for her, as much as I liked George . . . She was such a helpless little thing.' And I'd say, yes, I remembered her. I'd say, 'I often wonder what happened to her, too.' Other times he might say, 'You know, I still think about George Carlson. Do you remember how he was always running away when we were kids? Do you remember the time he stole old man Saint's boat and actually got halfway to Connecticut before they picked him up?' Then he'd shake his head, but he'd be half-smiling. 'Do you think he really

136

settled down with that woman he went off with – or do you think he left her, too? A man like that . . .'

But I never wondered about what had happened to George.

After I said goodbye to Lettie, I decided to walk down to the harbour for a while. It was there that George Carlson stole the boat to go to Connecticut when he was twelve. And it was there, nearly twenty-five years later, that James found Ann Carlson and the baby driving round and round the parking lot at one in the morning when he was coming back from delivering twins out at the hospital.

There were some men down at the water, fishing or working on their boats, and some children in the playground, but otherwise the park was empty. I sat down on a bench on the dock and looked out across the bay. All along the coast the trees were tall and green, but every so often you could see a car flash down the road. There were three sailboats heading out towards the Sound, cutting through the still water like fish, and everything that wasn't green or gold was blue. It was hard to imagine the bay frozen solid, the shoreline rounded by snow. But Lettie was right, that was the winter of the big freeze. It started snowing right before Christmas and didn't stop until Easter. People would say things like, 'I can't wait till the spring so I can see my front yard again,' and some kids whited out the word 'town' on the sign out by the old highway and painted in 'freezer' so it said 'Welcome to Harborside, the North Shore's First Freezer' (just the sort of thing George Carlson himself would have done). That was the winter James taught me to play backgammon and the Junior Auxiliary had a quilting bee; the winter Leroy Kennedy skied across the harbour because he was bored; the winter George Carlson ran away with his mistress and Ann, when she'd recovered, took her little girl and went back home.

If Ann Carlson is still alive, she'd be about my age now – on what the new doctor calls the rocky side of seventy – but I still see her as a young woman, not pretty, maybe, but sweet-looking, gentle. Too plain to be any trouble, as my father would have said. The sort of woman made for marriage – you could see that in the way she'd stand on her porch, in the way she'd march down the street on her way to the stores. In the beginning, you hardly ever saw her without him, walking along with her arm through his, like she was the moon and he was the sun. In the end, you never saw her that you didn't think of him – wondering where he was; wondering whether that was what she was wondering too. And even when the shouting began it was all his – his anger, his rage – no one ever heard her raise her voice. He might blame her for everything from the weather to his own unhappiness, but she never defended herself. For all the gossip, there was never anything said against her. No one ever suggested she deserved it. Or that she'd caused it. No one even called her a fool. Oh, someone might make some remark like, 'I'd never let my husband treat me like that,' or, 'She shouldn't let him walk all over her like that,' but none of us were schoolgirls, after all, we all knew what marriage was about.

The first time I saw Ann, she was walking down Main Street on George's arm, and I was standing on the front porch, waiting for the kids to get home from school. I was looking up the street the way they'd be coming, expecting to see them any minute – David walking slightly ahead,

Beth hurrying to keep up with him – but instead I saw
what I took to be lovers, deep in conversation as they
strolled along, their arms around each other's waists. The
town was just beginning to expand then, to get shopping
centres and housing developments, and I thought they
must be newcomers, escaping all the troubles of the city.
And then he laughed at something she said, leaning his
head back and whooping loudly, just like a kid. Don't be
ridiculous, I told myself, he's dead. Because by then, of
course, we all assumed that he was dead. It had been the
town prediction: he'll end bad. 'If you could eat charm,
he'd never go hungry, that one,' Lettie's mother used to
joke. But my mother put it differently: 'If he was in the
Garden of Eden you can bet he'd be the snake.'

And then he noticed me, leaning against the porch
pillar, holding on to the railing, staring at them like they
were a parade or something, and his smile got even
brighter. I don't know if he called out my name or not. I
don't know if she turned to him and asked him who I
was, if she tugged on his arm. All I could think of was
how the sun was shining and how quiet everything
seemed all of a sudden as though somebody'd turned
down the sound. All I could think of was that I'd been so
sure he was dead, gone for good.

And then I spotted Beth and David coming down the
street behind them, swinging at each other with their
sweaters, and the world sort of started up again.

'Why, George Carlson,' I said, starting down the stairs.
'George Carlson, I'd recognise you anywhere. You
haven't changed a bit.'

He laughed again, coming towards me, pulling her
with him. 'The prodigal returns,' he grinned.

If anything, he was better looking than he'd been as a
boy. Broader, more solid. The edginess and aggression

were gone, replaced by what I guessed was contentment. He stood there with his arm around her and his snappy brown suit and his gold rings and his shoes shining like mirrors. The hunger had been replaced by prosperity.

'This'll give the good folk of Harborside something to talk about, won't it, Louise? I bet everybody thought I was in prison – but here I am, with my new wife, all ready to settle down for ever. Home for good. That'll set them back on their heels, won't it, Louise?' And he laughed so loud that the kids, who were just about to pass him on their way into the house, froze in their tracks.

'It sure will,' I said, smiling at her, his new wife. 'It sure will.'

Wouldn't it just.

There's always a lot of talk about small towns and small town minds, as though people in them have nothing better to do than sit around spying on each other all day, wishing each other ill. George had certainly always felt like that about Harborside. For as long as I'd known him (from about four on) he'd always acted like the whole town was against him, that they wanted nothing more than to see him fail. It was as though his wildness was a reaction to the neatness and quiet of the streets, the virtuous predictability of our lives; as though it was all a challenge to him. 'They all hate me,' he'd say. 'They can't wait to see the back of me.' But that wasn't true. It was just that the rest of us knew who we were, knew where we stood. Of all the people I grew up with, George Carlson was the only one who had what he called 'big dreams'. 'Don't you want to get out of this town, Louise?' he'd ask me – maybe we'd be sitting down by the water or walking home from school, and I'd already be thinking

140

of what my mother's kitchen would smell like when I got there, what she'd say when I came through the back door. 'Don't you want to do things? See the world?' But I'd known exactly what I would do; what part of the world I wanted to see. I was going to stay in Harborside and get married, and I was going to have five children, three boys and two girls (I had three, one girl); I was going to live in a large old house on a shady street and I was going to teach Sunday school and in the winter my husband and I were going to go somewhere warm for a week (which I think must've been something I'd seen in some movie). And I got all those things. But George had always wanted something more. 'These people and their boring respectability,' he'd say. 'They make me sick. Do they think this is living, Louise? Do you?' And the answer of course was, yes. Yes, they thought that was living. Yes, I did too.

But for all of that, when George came back, with a shiny green DeSoto, enough money for a house in town and the sort of wife no one had ever imagined he'd choose, the town welcomed him with open arms. I think everyone believed he must've changed, that he'd been saved. That he'd finally come to his senses. 'He was always bright,' they said. 'He was never really a bad boy – just a bit of a handful.' 'It was just something he had to get out of his system.' It never occurred to any of them that he'd only come back to prove something to himself, to show us up – that inside that handsome, successful man, who joined the Legion and the Kiwanis just like all the other men his age, was that angry boy, as hungry as ever, still crazy to find a way out. It didn't occur to me for a while, either.

When George Carlson left town the first time, still just

a boy, everybody said it was because he'd gotten some girl in trouble. I don't know which one. 'All the girls were sweet on him,' Lettie said. 'It was like moths to a flame.' We were sitting in the ice-cream parlour next to the movies, having a soda, and George was outside the window, talking to one of the women from the new development. She looked like she'd come from the city. 'Don't you remember?'

'All the girls were afraid of him,' I said. 'That's what I remember. The nice girls had all been warned away. There wasn't one of them would have been caught dead talking to him.'

'Maybe,' Lettie said, taking a mouthful of ice cream. 'Maybe not. You were pretty fond of him yourself, if I remember correctly.'

'Don't be ridiculous, Lettie.' I'd taken the change for my soda out of my purse, but I couldn't get it to close again. 'We were like brother and sister, you know that.'

The Carlsons lived across the street from us when I was growing up, in an old yellow house with a screened-in porch and a weeping willow in the front yard. Their house always needed painting. My father said that was because they didn't own it, like we owned ours, but only rented it from a man in Albany. That was just one of the differences between the Carlsons and us.

Despite those differences, though, George and I became fast friends. He was six months younger than I was, a year behind in school. With the exception of my sister, he is the first other child I can remember – there for sleigh riding and tea parties; there when I learned how to jump rope, when I learned how to skate, when I learned how to ride a two-wheeler. Always there. I suppose my parents thought the friendship would just wear itself out as we got older, that the differences between us would set there like a wall. And in a way I guess they did. But it was a wall we learned to climb over, to go around. We went our separate ways (I had my crowd in high school, he quit and started working for Mr Sormani in the pharmacy). So that my mother could say to me, 'I never see that Carlson boy any more. Is he still in town?' and I could answer, 'As far as I know. We don't travel in the same circles.' But sometimes we would meet – almost by accident. Sometimes he would appear as I was coming out of the library on a spring evening, or as I was going home from the movies, on those last two blocks after I'd said goodbye to my friends. Sometimes, on a Saturday afternoon, I'd find him at the lake, fishing, or up in the woods at that old graveyard, his back against a stone. One night, when it was raining, we sat on the dock for hours, on that same bench I sat on the other day – and it was almost as though we were on a ship, on a ship out at sea. 'Mrs Hulahan said she saw George Carlson downtown, drunk as a lord in broad daylight,' my mother said. 'Doesn't surprise me,' said my father. 'Doesn't surprise me at all.' And one spring James Lethbridge came back from college and asked me to wear his pin. And I said, Yes, of course; there was no surprise in that, either.

At first George started stopping by on behalf of Ann. Could I introduce her to some of my friends? He knew how active I was, how many groups and committees I belonged to – could I take her along with me now and then? She was a very quiet person, he said, very reserved, but she was lonely; lonely and homesick. 'She misses Illinois,' he said. Then laughed, 'Though God knows there's nothing there to miss.' She had no gift for making friends, he said. Left to herself that was how she would stay. And in time not only did Ann and I strike up a friendship – walking to the Junior Auxiliary on Monday nights together, driving into Huntford for shopping and lunch, stopping by each other's house for a cup of coffee when we were passing – but the Carlsons and the Lethbridges became a foursome as well.

We went to the movies together, on picnics, out to dinner to celebrate a birthday or an anniversary. One summer we even went to the Catskills for two weeks, playing pinochle and drinking beer around an old tin-top table, betting pretzels, our voices the only sounds you could hear above the silence of the night. I still have the picture James took of the three of us, browned and smiling – George in the middle with his arms around our shoulders, me and Ann leaning forward, looking at each other around him. It was the only time James ever did any cooking, out at the side of the cabin on one of those portable grills, yelling at the mosquitoes, 'Aren't these darn things supposed to stay away from smoke, Louise?' And George would even help with the cleaning up sometimes, coming into the kitchen when I was washing the dishes, standing on the other side of the sink with that old checked cloth in his hands, talking while we worked and Ann made the coffee. Ann and I would go for walks while the men went fishing and the kids swam in the lake. We always carried one of those enamel saucepans in case we found any berries, and we'd just walk and walk and walk until we couldn't go any farther, until it seemed like we'd never get back.

That was when she first started to really talk to me. About Illinois, where she'd grown up. About meeting George, back wounded from the war. 'Everybody thought he was going to die,' she said. 'Everybody but me.' She told me how he'd tell her stories while she sponged him clean, while she helped him dress, while she rolled him over to change the sheets. 'Sometimes,' she said, 'when he was telling me his plans and things, he'd get this look in his eyes – like he was on fire inside.' She'd never met anyone like him before. On the night he proposed, he took her out to the river, kneeling in the moonlight, promising the world at her feet. But all she ever wanted was him – him and some kids and a place of their own.

'I don't know what I can do,' she said. 'I'd do anything, I try everything . . . but nothing's enough. It'll never be enough.'

We were sitting on the lakeshore, watching the men row the kids back from the store on the other side. They were singing some song about a sailor.

'Don't be ridiculous,' I said. 'You're a good wife, what more can you be?'

She waved to the kids, who were calling our names, turning her face away from me. 'I wish I knew.'

For some minutes we sat there, watching the little rowboat, painted bright blue, and the men, each wearing swim trunks, a T-shirt and a canvas fisherman's hat, their oars cutting into the water with assurance and determination. The sun was on them and they were smiling, almost looking as though they were returning from some victory, some danger. If you'd been passing by and had seen them, that's what you'd have thought: there go two men in a boat, maybe out for a little fishing, a little hunting, a little exploring, maybe just teaching their children to row. You wouldn't have been able to tell anything else about them – that James was a doctor and George a salesman, that James belonged to the Rotary and liked his eggs cooked for exactly three minutes, that George had been Salesman of the Year three years running and always spit-shined his shoes. You'd have thought them capable of anything, men of potential. And if you'd seen me and

Ann, in our pedal pushers and bright summer shirts, one eye always on the boat and its occupants, you'd have thought: And those must be their wives.

She picked up a stone and threw it into the lake. 'I sure wish I knew.'

But by then Ann wasn't the only one who was talking. People were saying that George sometimes came back early from his business trips and instead of going home he stayed at the hotel over in Huntford, fifteen miles away, that he drank too much and wasn't alone. Someone said they'd seen him in the city with a blonde, or on the train from the city with a redhead, or sneaking into Maureen Tabor's house (Maureen was our only divorcee) on a weekday night. All of a sudden it seemed that everyone had a George Carlson story – what he'd done, what he'd said, what he was rumoured to have done or said. Just like when he was a boy. He'd started fighting with Ann so the neighbours could hear it, could hear him slam out of the house and into the car, hear him roar down the road, Ann standing at the front door, crying like a little girl. And then Ann Carlson had a baby girl. 'That should keep him at home,' said Lettie. There were about six of us cleaning up after a church supper when Lettie said that, but not one of us looked up, said a word. We were all probably thinking it was already too late.

And by then, of course, George was talking to me too. In a way we just picked up where we'd left off. It started with him dropping by when he was passing, or offering me a lift if he met me down at the A & P. And pretty soon we were arranging to meet, out of everyone's way – not to do anything, you understand, but just to be together, just to talk, just like we used to. By then I suppose he was drinking too much and maybe even running around, but we never spoke about that. Sometimes we'd go into Huntford, to the movies, eating pop corn and Milk Duds and giggling like kids. I'd say it was harmless – I told myself it was harmless – but of course it wasn't, it was the most dangerous thing I'd ever done. I'd say it was nobody's business, but of course it was. Sometimes he would call me up from some hotel in Pittsburgh or Albany or Jersey City. 'I just want to hear your voice, Louise,' he'd say. 'I just want to hear your voice.'

George Carlson wanted me to go away with him. We'd go to Canada or to California. We'd start all over again. With me everything would be different. But there was Ann. And there was James and my kids and my garden with its pansies and its lilies and its Canterbury Bells. Sometimes at night I'd lie awake, James snoring in the next bed, and I'd try to imagine what would happen if I really did leave. How the house would sound at night without me; what the children would look like, how their voices would echo when they came home from school and I wasn't there. How James's footsteps would climb the stairs from his office if I wasn't there to hear them, to call out to him. How it would feel to kiss, to touch another man. But I couldn't do it; couldn't imagine what a new life would be like, how it would be different, what it might be worth. 'Do you think just because a man has a family and a steady job and shaves twice a day that he stops living . . . that he stops wanting things?' George would ask me. 'Is this all there is – this house, this street, these people, and then you die?' And sometimes when he said things like that, sometimes when we were out together, just driving around, I'd almost be able to feel what more you could want, almost be able to imagine myself as someone else. Nearly.

James found Ann and the baby driving around in the

parking lot by the harbour at about one in the morning. In the summertime, that's where the teenagers always hang out, sitting in the shadows drinking out of bottles wrapped in paper bags, laughing suddenly, but that night it was empty. It had started snowing around midnight, small flakes clinging to each tree, each building, the quiet streets, the green DeSoto going round and round in a lunar landscape. She wasn't crying then, James said, she was just cutting circles in the snow, her lights out and the baby sound asleep beside her. He recognised the car instantly, got out of our old Mercury and went over and flagged her down. 'Ann,' he said. 'Ann, what's wrong?' 'Hello, James,' she said. 'What are you doing here?' She had her blue winter coat on over her pyjamas and robe and a pair of those slippers made out of wash cloths. When he asked her where George was she kept repeating the name over and over. 'George? George? George?' – as though she wasn't sure who he meant. And then she began to cry. Then she told James how George had come home drunk and told her he was leaving; how they'd had this big fight. How he'd said there was someone else. 'Not one of those sluts they all talk about him being with,' she said – James was surprised to hear her say that word, slut, how unnatural it sounded coming from her – 'not one of his whores. Someone he loved.' And then he went. He said they were going off together, he and this woman, this woman who made him feel so alive, going off to have a real life, real passion. He packed his bag and he went. He didn't even want to see the baby one last time, plant one last kiss on that tiny face, he just went. And Ann put the baby in her snowsuit and got into the car and drove around and around, maybe thinking she would find George, that she would find him and persuade him to come back. Drove around, crazy with grief.

Nobody was surprised. Everybody agreed that she was better off without him. 'I loved him so much,' she said to me, her eyes on the air around us. 'I loved him so.' Everybody said it was just her pride was hurt. 'She's still young,' they said. 'She'll find someone else.' After Christmas, Ann went back home and the house was sold, and that spring I got pregnant with Jimmy, what James always joked was our 'little afterthought'.

I'd been waiting for him that night. For George. I'd packed my suitcase and unpacked it and packed it and unpacked it again. And I was waiting for him, for his knock on the back door, so I could tell him that I couldn't do it, I couldn't go. Not even for him. Life wasn't like that. I wasn't like that.

What really happened? I wonder. Were they fighting and she hit him with something? Maybe he was so drunk he fell down the stairs, his brown leather suitcase banging behind him. Did she push him as he turned his back on her. Did he simply stumble, in such a hurry that he missed his footing? She would have been able to put him into the car through the garage, which led straight into the house. No one would have seen her. And after that?

While James was putting her to bed that night, giving her a sedative, talking to her in his gentle voice, I went out to bring her car into the driveway. George's suitcase was still in the trunk. She must have forgotten it. It must have gone right out of her mind. It was nearly five by then, but it was snowing heavily and there was no one about. If anyone saw me take the suitcase out of the trunk and carry it into the house, what could they have thought? They would have thought, there's Louise Lethbridge, prancing around in the snow at five in the morning, busy even at this hour, getting ready to wake up the house and fix her husband's breakfast and get her kids off to school, what a good wife.

But I'd been waiting that night – I guess I've always been waiting.

Pandik

D W Smith

A youngish man – thirty, perhaps, wearing overalls – got out of a van and looked up and down the prosperous street near Primrose Hill. He sniffed. Anybody watching might have thought he took longer than was really necessary to check the address of the house by which he'd parked. Given the neighbourhood, the watcher might well have thought that was typical of today's working man. The man got back in the van and drove into the semi-circular driveway hidden by a high hedge between two gates. Any witness would have been more surprised if it had been possible to see the second man who came out of the rear doors. They made an odd pair – the one in overalls, blond, untidy hair, about five feet nine, appropriate to his van which bore the name of a plumbing company on the side; the other, several inches taller, dark hair sleekly brushed, wearing an elegantly cut suit. At the handsome front door the smaller one rang the bell.

'Mr Croft?' said the taller one when the door was opened. 'I'm Detective Chief Inspector Fathers. This is Detective Sergeant Yarrow.'

The man at the door stood aside to let them in, casting an eye at the detective sergeant's overalls.

'Excuse his get-up,' said Fathers. 'It goes with the van: a mild disguise, just in case anybody's watching.'

'They're not,' Yarrow commented as he closed the door behind him.

George Croft led the two detectives into a large, sunlit lounge. 'My wife, Jennifer,' he said. 'Chief Inspector Fathers. Sergeant Yarrow.'

'We've just finished breakfast,' his wife responded, 'but there's more coffee. Will you take some? I'll get it. We normally have somebody, but not just now.'

'Please sit down,' Croft said as his wife left.

'Still no word?' asked Fathers, trying to sit comfortably at one end of the long, cold, leather-covered sofa. 'At the moment, the main thing is to sit and wait for their call. Somebody's down at the school now to check up on the car. And, of course, we're keeping a constant ear on your telephone.'

Jennifer Croft returned with the coffee tray. She poured out and offered biscuits. She perched beside her husband on the matching sofa opposite Fathers, at whom she beamed a strangely bright smile. 'Is this a Scotland Yard case now?' she asked.

'Yes, though the local CID will continue on it, working with us,' Fathers replied. 'They called us because of certain features of what happened last time which relate to one of our long-term enquiries.' In return for this non-communication, Jennifer Croft gave him another smile.

'Before we get on to that,' Fathers continued, 'let's be clear about what's happened this time. Yesterday, I gather, Peter was meant to go to a friend's and return here about six-thirty. When he didn't, you called and found out he hadn't been there. You then phoned the police.'

'That's right,' said George Croft. 'Bess – that's the friend – said she'd seen him getting into a big grey car outside the school. Apparently her damn mother didn't think to call to make sure it was all right.'

'He always goes home with Bess on a Tuesday,' Jennifer Croft added. 'But then he didn't last week either, so maybe Steph thought when he wasn't there, the arrangement was off.'

'And maybe she just didn't bloody think at all,' observed George Croft.

'Well, it wouldn't have done any good if she had phoned – we were neither of us here.'

Her husband snorted. 'I find it incredible,' he said, 'after what happened last week. Peter's not stupid, and anyway he's been brought up on saying no to strangers and all that.'

'What time did you get home yesterday?'

'Well, I got home at six-ish,' said Jennifer Croft, 'and George was here about, what . . .?'

'Half-six,' said George Croft.

'Oh, I thought it was closer to seven.'

'Half-six,' her husband repeated.

'Oh.'

'And when did you call about Peter?' asked Fathers.

'Almost straight away,' George Croft replied.

'Oh, no, we really waited quite a while,' said his wife. 'Well, he's often late back from Steph's. You know, you make these arrangements but they're never kept to the exact minute, are they?'

'Of course not,' said Fathers. 'So when was the call made?'

'Oh, about half-past seven, I should think.'

George Croft shrugged irritably. 'Maybe,' he said. 'Thought it was earlier, but maybe.'

Fathers put his cup and saucer down on the coffee table. The discrepancies in their recollections were irrelevant. Presumably the husband realised that what his wife said – which was probably the truth – did not reveal a high sense of parental responsibility. Well, that was the Crofts' problem, not his. A more sinister explanation was unlikely.

'Right,' he said, 'tell me about the time before. I know you've described it already, but I hope you won't mind repeating it. You didn't call the police then – when was it? – a week ago last Sunday – did you?'

'That's right,' Croft replied. 'I judged it safer that way.'

'They didn't ask for too terribly much, after all,' his wife said. 'And we did get him back, didn't we?'

'But now,' said her husband, 'they've got him again and it's got to stop. That's why this time I called the police immediately. We can't go on tossing the boy and ten thousand pounds backwards and forwards every week, can we? Like blackmail. Once it starts, you never pay them off.'

'That's your experience, is it?' said Fathers. His voice was expressionless, but Yarrow slurped a suppressed chuckle into his coffee.

'Well – I mean, in the books and films and so on,' explained Croft. 'That's how it always seems to work, doesn't it?'

'It all went so smoothly, you see,' Jennifer Croft said. 'George did as they said, and home he came. We kept him off school the rest of the week, and then popped down to Brighton for the weekend, but he went back to school as normal this week – because there was no real trouble about it. Except that he was kidnapped, I mean.' Her cheeks reddened with her confusion and she sipped some coffee to collect herself. Before she could emphasise

154

that she didn't mean that having her ten-year-old son kidnapped was not real trouble, Fathers asked how it happened.

George Croft gave a crisp account. Anne-Marie, the *au pair*, had taken Peter for a walk after lunch. While she was reading and he was playing around in and out the trees a small boy brought her a note. It read simply, 'The boy's safe. Call home.' She ran after the boy and asked where he got the note. 'A man' and 'He give me a quid' were all she understood of his reply. She hunted for Peter in case it was one of his pranks. By the time she phoned the Crofts, they'd received a call telling them they could have Peter back, unharmed, for ten thousand pounds in cash. They had to get it by noon on Tuesday when they would be phoned again.

'Where's Anne-Marie, by the way?' Fathers interrupted.

'Gone,' said George Croft shortly.

'Gone?'

'Yes. What d'you expect? Bloody irresponsible fool of a girl. I gave her a month's money and she left on Monday. Afternoon, was it, Jen?'

'She did leave a forwarding address,' said Jennifer Croft.

'We'd like it. And her full name and home address.'

'I've got it upstairs somewhere.'

George Croft continued, 'You've been told, I suppose, that first thing on Monday I hired a private enquiry agency.'

'Yes – Douglas and Jenks, isn't it? Have you used them before?'

'No. I heard about them from a friend who – well, they handled a personal problem very well for him, tactfully and discreetly. I remembered the name and found the number in the directory.'

'Who'd you see there?'

'Jenks. And he called in a chap called Robinson who ended up by agreeing to act as a sort of go-between. Well, he offered and I accepted. It was a relief.'

Croft paused. He seemed to want affirmation that it was all right to have needed that sort of relief. 'Mm,' said Fathers, obligingly.

'Then I went to the bank to arrange for the money to be ready on Tuesday morning.'

'Were you asked why you wanted so much cash?'

'Yes. At Robinson's suggestion, I said I needed it to buy a car.'

'Go on.'

'Tuesday, Robinson came with me to get the money. We came back here, and at noon precisely a man phoned. He was in a call-box at a station. Or maybe an airport. I thought I could hear loudspeaker announcements. I asked if Peter was all right, and he said, Yes, and asked if I had the money, and I said, Yes. Then I said I hadn't called the police but I'd got somebody with me I wanted to handle it, and he said to put him on.'

'Did he sound angry, or ruffled, or put out at all? Surprised?'

Croft thought for a while and then said, 'No. None of those things.'

'Did you by any chance tape the conversation?'

'Robinson did, with one of those things in a briefcase where you fix the mike on to the handset.'

Fathers turned to Yarrow. 'Skipper, use the phone in the van to call this Robinson and get him down the local nick.' Yarrow nodded and went out thinking dark, unfriendly thoughts. Fathers asked Croft to continue.

'Well, Robinson said who he was and that he'd follow the instructions, stressed that I wanted to cooperate fully

156

and the money was there. I had the impression he was implying he would handle it more smoothly than I could, which I suppose is probably true, but he didn't use those exact words, you see, as if he thought I'd mind if he came straight out with it.'

Which I suppose is probably true, thought Fathers.

'When he'd finished he told me he had to collect Peter at five in Hyde Park. And that was it. That's what happened. He left at four with the money and arrived back with Peter about six.'

'So, as you said, Mrs Croft, it all went very smoothly,' said Fathers. 'And then they went and did it again.' He drummed his fingers on his knee. 'Do you think you could get the address Anne-Marie left with you, please, Mrs Croft? And her home address in wherever it is – France?'

Jennifer Croft rose. 'Belgium,' she said.

'And a photograph of your son – recent one, of course. And when you come back, I'd like to know what Peter was wearing yesterday.'

Fathers got up too and stretched to ease his back; the sofa had forced him into a slump which left a pain from his neck to the base of his spine. He walked to the french windows and looked out at the large garden. It was a sunny, late September day, beginning to get warm enough to justify his choice of summer-weight suit that morning, the last fling before autumn proper set in. George Croft joined him. He stood right beside the tall detective and looked up at him. 'Do you have any idea who it is?' he asked.

Fathers took a step backwards, an instinctive reaction, not to the question, but to the other man's proximity. He shrugged. 'Not their names,' he said. He pondered silently. His section was investigating a series of kidnappings.

What happened the first time Peter Croft was kidnapped fitted a familiar pattern. The second one didn't. It was the first case he knew of where the gang had repeated the trick. He wondered why and stared moodily down the garden at the perfect flowerbeds.

Behind them, the door opened. Yarrow entered. 'You won't believe this,' he said.

He stepped aside. Behind him was Detective Sergeant Gordon. Fathers looked at her and opened his mouth to ask what the hell she thought she was up to, coming to the target's house so openly, risking being spotted by the kidnappers. She raised one hand to stop him and reached behind herself with the other to pull forward a person wearing a grey blazer with pink trim over white shirt, pink and grey tie, grey shorts. A small person who looked very reluctant, rather sheepish, but a little defiant. A ten-year-old boy who kept hold of Detective Sergeant Gordon's hand and gave every sign of wanting to hide behind her raincoat again, and who did not run to his father who was standing awkwardly on the other side of the room.

They stood looking at each other.

'Where have you been?' George Croft finally asked. His son looked at him. Said nothing.

Jennifer Croft pushed past the two detectives at the door. She put her hand on her son's shoulder. 'Darling, where have you been?' she said.

Peter looked up and met his mother's eyes. 'I'm all right,' he said.

'But where have you been?' repeated the father.

'Really,' said Peter, 'I am all right.'

Fathers jerked his chin at Cathy Gordon who extricated her hand from Peter's grip and squeezed into the hallway, Yarrow following, past Jennifer Croft as she again asked Peter where he'd been. 'My God, we've been so worried,' she said.

'Honestly, I'm quite all right,' he replied. He was doing his best to be reassuring with a voice which quavered as he became more insistent.

Fathers spoke to George Croft in an undertone. 'We'll go now,' he said, 'except for DS Gordon. I suggest you get a doctor.'

'He says he's all right,' George Croft said.

'He may be saying that precisely because he's not. Have him change out of those clothes and keep them for us. I'll see you shortly.'

Croft nodded uncertainly. 'Where have you been, though?' he asked again.

On his way out, Fathers relieved Jennifer Croft of a slip of paper. She smiled vaguely as she let go of it. Anne-Marie's forwarding and family addresses were written on it. In the hallway, he asked Cathy Gordon the Crofts' question. 'He was at school,' she replied. 'Bright as a button till we got here. I didn't have time to get anything on the car.'

He sighed and told her to wait till the doctor came. He was interrupted as George Croft repeated the refrain – 'Where have you been?' – with the volume and violence of a parade-ground roar. Fathers looked at the ground and shook his head sadly. 'Good luck, Cath,' he said.

'Would you bloody believe it?' asked Yarrow. They were in a featureless office at the police station, made free for them to use as a situation room.

'They're not bad people,' said Fathers, 'just not very good parents, not in these circumstances anyway.'

'Tough time,' acknowledged Yarrow, 'but even so . . .'

'Even so,' Fathers conceded. 'Now, find yourself a

motor and get on to this Anne-Marie person. Check the account of the snatch, alibi her for yesterday and get what background you can on the family.'

'Alibi?' said Yarrow pointedly. Fathers shrugged and gave him a look. The detective sergeant shrugged back and wandered off to negotiate a car.

Fathers phoned the Crofts' house. Cathy Gordon answered. 'He's still not saying where he was last night,' she said quietly. 'They've bullied him, cajoled, bribed – all he says is he's all right. The doc'll be round in a bit. The clothes are ready.'

'Do you think you're going to get anything out of the kid?'

'No, frankly. If he wasn't terrified before, he is now. Mister carried on for a while in the same tone you heard, and the boy clammed up entirely. She's just as bad as her husband, too.'

'Huh. Stay there till the doctor's finished, grab the clothes and get back down to the school about the car. Maybe we'll see the Crofts again this afternoon. See if you can't get them to let it lie for a while.'

'I don't think restraint is their strong point.'

'Do your best.'

Fathers hung up, leaned back in his chair, put his feet on the desk, and wondered how he'd react if one of his children were kidnapped. A knock on the door disturbed his reflections. As he flicked his feet to the floor and sat up straight, a uniformed sergeant showed in a smartly dressed man in his early thirties. It was Robinson from the Douglas and Jenks Agency. Fathers introduced himself.

Robinson sat down. 'You're Serious Crimes, aren't you? How can I help?'

'It's about the Croft kidnapping.'

Robinson raised his eyebrows to express polite puzzlement.

160

'It's OK, Mr Robinson. George Croft told us about it this morning.'

'Oh. He told me he wouldn't tell anybody, not even the boy's school.'

'That may've been his intention. But Peter didn't come home from school last night, and this time he decided to call the police.'

Robinson opened his mouth, then snapped it shut and stayed silent. A frown passed across his face and was replaced by more polite puzzlement.

'The boy's all right,' Fathers continued. 'He was back at school this morning. Right now he's at home with a doctor giving him the once over.'

'So – I don't understand, I'm afraid.'

'Peter wasn't seen from the end of school yesterday until this morning. We're filling in the details now. He wasn't with his parents last night, that's the key thing.'

'And they called the police?'

'Of course.'

'Has he said where he was?'

'Not so far. He was seen getting into a car after school. We're trying to get a description now.'

'Seen by other kids, you mean?'

'Yeah.'

'How is he?'

Fathers shrugged. 'Says he's all right. The doctor will tell us about that. Seems he was pretty cheerful at school. Not so cheerful now, though.'

Robinson pouted with incomprehension. 'Very strange, isn't it?' he said. 'Doesn't really sound like kidnapping, in fact.'

Fathers shrugged again. 'If the parents say whoever he was with had no permission to take him off, a kidnapping charge'd probably stick.'

161

'Mm, well, legal fine points aren't my department, I'm afraid. I suppose you want to talk about last week.'

With that, Robinson dismissed Peter's second kidnapping and launched into an account of the first one. From Croft's arrival at Douglas and Jenks to the phone call at noon on the Tuesday, it matched what Fathers had already been told. Robinson's instructions were to be on the north side of the Carriage Road just before Rotten Row at five exactly, on foot, with his car parked at least a hundred yards away, and the money in a briefcase.

'Then I got the usual warning about no funny business, no police, no marked notes – all that. The bloke said they could and would pick Peter up again any time they wanted if there was any trouble. I swore there'd be none and that was that. So I had lunch with Croft and hung around till four while he did some paperwork. He was still busy when I left.'

Fathers doodled an intricate geometric design on his pad. 'Paperwork,' he said, 'while you got his son after two days with a load of kidnappers.'

'Sounds weird, doesn't it? But different people have different ways of reacting to stress. One of his ways was to go on about how much time this was costing him. Didn't seem to give a toss about the ten grand. It was the hours of work he was losing which bothered him. Takes all sorts.'

'That's how it seems. So you got to the Carriage Road?'

'Where I waited about ten minutes. A nondescript Datsun pulls up. I hold up the briefcase. A hand stretches out from the front window and snatches it. The rear door opens and out tumbles the boy. It didn't take more'n a couple of seconds and off they go – no squealing tyres and such-like, but they got away smartish.'

'See any faces?'

162

'No. Peter told me afterwards there were three of them, all wearing masks. Sounded like the kind motorcyclists wear in winter.'

'Car number?'

'At the office.'

'I'll want the recording you made of your phone conversation.'

'Also at the office. You're welcome to it.'

Fathers looked up from his doodles. 'What do you think about them, then?'

'Very professional,' said Robinson. 'In an area like this, you get a few kidnappings and we get called in now and again, so we've developed a bit of experience.' He checked the points off on his fingers: 'Clean snatch to begin with. Not an outrageously high ransom. Minimal contact with target. Very fast exchange. Didn't even bother to check the money, you see: the warning's been given and they know we know they can grab the kid again if we've not played straight. Plus being happy to have a third party involved, which makes sense for them, especially if it's a kid they've snatched. Parents are apt to do stupid things. Last and not least, the victim's back in one piece. All the signs. Have you come across them before?'

'Let's say the pattern's familiar. All the points you've mentioned. We might turn out to be very grateful for that recording of yours. One other thing, Mr Robinson. How was Peter when you drove him home?'

'Eh? Oh, he was fine, fine. Plucky little beggar, really. Full of chat about it all. Said he'd been scared. He knew what was happening, all right. But he said the men treated him pretty well . . .'

'He said they were all men, did he?'

'Well, he didn't mention any women.'

163

'Go on. They treated him pretty well.'

'Fed him on burgers and beans and had a telly there for him to watch. Said they told him right from the start that he'd be home soon, his father was going to pay up. Obviously he was lonely and everything, but the thing which bothered him most was that they kept their masks on all the time. Wanted to know who I was and what I did. I gave him my card, actually, and he put it away very carefully.' Robinson chuckled.

'You liked him.'

'Yeah, he's a nice, bright kid – very likeable.'

'Did he have any idea where he was held?'

'All he knew was it was half an hour's drive, because of the exchange point. He knew that from the programme he was watching when they came to get him. Otherwise, nothing. Small room, no windows, just a telly and a bed, with a loo and wash-hand basin in the corner. Said he never heard any noise from outside so he supposed it was properly soundproofed.'

'Did he, indeed?'

Robinson chuckled again.

'And how was it when you got him back to the house?' Fathers asked.

Robinson's face clouded. He became apologetic, defensive. 'It's not easy,' he said, 'not easy for the parents, situation like that.'

'You mean it wasn't nice.'

'Well, it's like when a little boy hurts himself falling off a wall and his mother wants to comfort him but because she's alarmed and anxious it comes out wrong. They wanted to say how happy they were he was back all safe and sound, and it came out as saying he shouldn't've run off and played like that out of the *au pair's* sight, and then they started shouting about what an irresponsible bitch

164

she was and how you shouldn't use language like that in front of Peter. No, it wasn't very nice. They were confused.'

'Ho-hum,' said Fathers, bored by Robinson's pop psychology and depressed by the familiarity of it all, 'thanks for your time, anyway. Perhaps you'd phone through the number of that Datsun when you get back to your office. We'll drop round to collect the tape.'

When Robinson had left, the desk sergeant phoned up to say that Cathy Gordon had left a message for Fathers. She was on her way to Peter Croft's school. The doctor had not found even minor cuts and bruises, let alone serious injuries or, as the message put it, 'any real nastiness'. Then Yarrow phoned. He'd had no trouble finding Anne-Marie. She had been upset about the kidnapping and about the treatment she'd received from Mr Croft. She had what seemed a strong alibi for the previous afternoon and evening and Yarrow wanted to know what to do after he'd checked it out.

'You think she's pukka then, do you?' Fathers asked.

'That's the way it looks, Guv. Says she was at an employment agency in the afternoon, and went to the theatre with a friend in the evening. Not difficult to break if it's not for real.'

'No. Get any background? What's she think of the family?'

'Not a lot.'

'So tell me who does.'

'She says they're nice enough people but with a strictly limited amount of time and energy for the boy. Apparently he gets bored a lot, and they don't listen to him. Don't really know what he's interested in, don't hear out his stories about school and so on, don't listen to his problems.'

'An average family.'

Yarrow grunted. 'The way she put it is the boy has a good spirit. She says he's got a lot to survive but he'll come through. Obviously fond of him, but it seems she found it pretty hard, because he wanted her to be like an aunty – needed her to be, maybe – while the Crofts treated her like a maid. She was the one he told his troubles to, and then, if she could, she'd grab a quick word with the mother and suggest a way to sort it out. Sounds like they've made a right difficult kid out of him. Full of pranks directed against his parents. Not vicious, but – well, it seems he was only happy when he was winding them up.'

'Good work. Do the alibi and get back here. If you run into any problems, call me.'

After they'd hung up, Robinson was on the line with the number of the Datsun. Fathers thanked him, made a phone call to confirm his assumption that it had been stolen, and then went to get a cup of tea in the canteen. As he sit drinking and reflecting, Cathy Gordon joined him.

'Got a make,' she said. 'No trouble. One of the other boys saw it. B-registered BMW, four-door saloon, silver-grey. Nothing on the stolen vehicles register – I called in on my way back.'

'Well, maybe I'll ask the computer to tell us everybody in the country who owns a car like that. Just for fun.'

'One thing I can't work out: why did they snatch him again? And having done that, why didn't they go through with it?'

'That's two things you can't work out,' Fathers corrected her.

'But it doesn't make sense, does it? Or does it?'

'I don't think the same lot picked him up again. Wrong pattern. They wouldn't make the grab like that, and even if they did they'd've boosted the motor first. I talked with Robinson about it, and it's clear that lot were real professionals. No, the real question isn't why or why not: it's who Peter was with last night.'

'Well, the answer to that is down to Peter.'

'Mm. When Yarrow gets back, we'll see if we can persuade the lad to tell us. Meantime, let's reflect on the upper-middle-class family in the late twentieth century.'

'How d'you like the car?' Yarrow asked.

Sitting beside him in the front seat, with the other two detectives in the back, Peter Croft grinned and nodded his head vigorously. 'It's great,' he said. 'Can you go really fast?'

'I don't see why not,' said the man who'd impressively introduced himself as Detective Chief Inspector Fathers from Scotland Yard.

Yarrow tugged at Peter's seat belt to check it was secure, then switched on the siren and lights, changed down a gear and accelerated past the cars in front. Peter leaned over to watch the speedometer zip up to sixty-five and nodded his approval. At traffic lights at a crossroads, Yarrow braked and nudged the car out on the wrong side of the refuge. The cars crossing in front stopped and made room. He swung the wheel hard right and accelerated sharply, creating a satisfyingly dramatic screech of tyres and flinging Peter against the door. Yarrow hauled him upright then tucked the car through a gap in the oncoming traffic and charged down a side street. Peter sat entranced at the power of the car, Yarrow's skill and the extraordinary influence of the lights and siren on all other road-users. Finally Fathers called a halt.

'That was great,' Peter said. 'Do you think – um, would you let me use the radio?'

'I don't think so,' Fathers said gently. 'Somebody might get annoyed.'

'Yes, I suppose you can't fill the air-waves up with just playing around,' Peter said, regretfully but responsibly. He thought he heard the woman detective in the back seat mutter something like, 'You'd be surprised,' but he wasn't sure. 'Still,' he added, 'thanks for turning on the speed and everything. It's great. Do you get to do that a lot?' He sounded as if he'd join the police there and then if the answer was yes.

'Some,' said Fathers. 'It depends.' Peter nodded, but did the woman say, 'At the drop of a hat'? Again, Peter wasn't sure.

'You know, Peter,' Fathers said, 'you really should tell us where you were last night.'

The boy's shoulders tightened. 'Is that why you brought me out in the car?' he asked accusingly.

'No, of course not,' Fathers lied. 'We just thought you'd like a spin. But you really should tell us.'

'I can't.'

'If you want,' Fathers offered, 'we won't tell your parents.'

Peter considered. 'I'm sorry,' he said, 'but I can't tell you.'

'Tell us, at least,' Cathy Gordon said, 'was it the same people who took you off last week?'

'Oh!' said Peter explosively. 'Oh, no, it wasn't them. Is that what you were thinking? No, it wasn't them.'

'Please, Peter,' said Fathers, 'who was it, then?'

'I'm sorry. I'd like to tell you but I can't. I really can't.'

Fathers opened his mouth to insist on getting the answer, but a frown from Cathy Gordon cut him off.

They talked about football and tennis the rest of the way back to Peter's house.

'Let's go through it once more,' said Fathers. They'd left Peter with his parents and were on the way to the offices of Douglas and Jenks to collect Robinson's tape. 'The boy's kidnapped. His parents pay up and get him back. A week later he disappears again, driven off after school in a car which isn't on the stolen vehicles' register. We can assume he's right it wasn't the same lot having another go at him. Next morning, at five to nine as ever, he's back at school, just like normal. No injuries. He won't say what happened however mean his parents are, however nice we are. Anything I missed?'

'Not unless the computer gives us something about owners of B-reg BMWs,' Cathy Gordon said.

'Why won't Peter say where he was?' asked Yarrow.

There was a long silence. Cathy Gordon broke it: 'Kids're like grown-ups,' she said. 'They keep quiet about something because they're scared, because they've been naughty, or because they like having secrets.'

'Scared's the most likely,' said Fathers. 'But by whom and why? And what've we got? A second kidnapping just by coincidence?'

Yarrow stopped the car. 'This looks like it, Guv,' he said. 'Through that gateway there. D'you want me to go?'

'No, it's OK. I'll get it.'

Fathers got out and disappeared through the gate. Yarrow turned in his seat to face Cathy Gordon. 'One thing,' he said. 'If the people who held Peter first time were masked, how'd he know it wasn't them last night?'

She looked at him with interest, but before she'd formed a guess to test on her younger colleague, their boss was back. He got into the car. 'Cracked it,' he said, 'I

169

think. Back to the station, Yarrer.'

As Yarrow started the car, Cathy Gordon asked, 'Are you going to let us in on it?'

'No, I don't think so. Then I won't look stupid if I'm wrong.'

'Oh, great. It's so nice to work with you and learn all the secrets of your phenomenal success – inspiring even.'

'Up yours too. Yarrer, tell me: when you talked to her, did the *au pair* ask how Peter was?'

'Um, no, I don't think she did. Why? Actually, I might not have given her a chance to, but I'm pretty sure she didn't ask herself.'

'OK. Drop me at the station and call on her again. I want to know what she did last week – especially, if she saw Peter. In fact, start with that question. If you draw a blank, get an hour by hour account. Cath, liberate a car for yourself and get back to the Crofts.'

'Oh, joy of joys.'

'You want the details of how Peter spent last week after he got home on Tuesday.'

It took her half an hour to get to the Crofts' house, talk to Jennifer Croft and report by phone to Fathers with obvious surprise at what she'd discovered. It didn't surprise him. It was another hour until Yarrow phoned. Fathers filled in the time, first by cancelling the computer search he'd requested for owners of silver-grey, four-door, B-registered BMWs, and next by calling his office to discuss the cases he'd left behind to come out on what, apart from Robinson's tape, he now regarded as a nonsense and a waste of time. By the time Yarrow phoned, Cathy Gordon had returned. She drove Fathers to Douglas and Jenks Ltd. In the lobby she flashed her warrant card and asked to see Robinson. The receptionist's routine prevarication forced Fathers' irritation to breaking point.

'Don't piss about,' he snapped. 'It's police business. Where is he?' In angry silence, the receptionist pointed at a door. He opened it and strode down a corridor till he found Robinson's nameplate and strode into the office. Cathy Gordon followed him quickly enough to catch the start of his tirade.

'You have caused a monumental waste of time. I am a senior police officer with better things to do than dance around in circles, and you, whatever you call your job, it's not social worker, child psychologist or family therapist. Cough now or I'll see you screwed.'

Robinson was apologetic and placatory. 'I'm really sorry I messed you about,' he said, 'but I didn't realise he hadn't told his parents. I guess I should've come clean when we spoke earlier, but it all took me a bit aback.'

With a single synaptic click, Cathy Gordon understood.

'I realise,' Robinson was saying, 'that I should've spoken to his parents, but – well, now I think of it, when Peter called me from Brighton he pretended his parents were in the room with him. He actually called out something like, He says it's all right, Mum. Cunning bugger.'

'One of his pranks,' Fathers said.

'I didn't know he'd done it till we were talking this morning – you and me. I just gave as little away as I could so I'd be able to think about my position later. It's not good, is it?'

'Ah, sod it,' said Fathers, his anger subsiding. 'I'm not going to mess around with it any more.'

'I also didn't want to hurt Peter,' Robinson explained. 'I mean, right there and then when we'd got him back, after they'd yelled at him for a while, they decided to keep him off school for the week, and the wife suddenly says it's all a bit inconvenient and who's going to look after Peter now Anne-Marie's not there. Says she can cover on Wednesday, but can't they get somebody for Thursday. So Peter just upped and asked me to take him to the zoo. I didn't have the heart to say no. And the old man immediately says he'll pay me at agency rates plus expenses, would you believe? When I collected Peter at the house, he'd found Anne-Marie's number, called her and roped her in too. So we picked her up and the three of us spent the day together. Had a grand time.'

'And you'd given him your card already, and that's how he called you on Sunday from Brighton.'

'Yeah, it has my home number on it. From what he said, I reckon he was bored in Brighton, found a quiet moment and fixed this whole thing up. Little bleeder might've found a way to get at his folks without landing me in it, though.' Robinson sounded affectionate, not angry.

Fathers rubbed a hand tiredly across his face. 'I gather Anne-Marie couldn't make it yesterday?'

'No. I called her. She had interviews at an employment agency in the afternoon, and a theatre booked for the evening. Well then, where are we now? You say you're not taking it any further.'

'I should find some godawful way of wasting your time, but I can't say I think it's your fault. Or Peter's, come to that. If you give me the tape, we'll be on our way.'

'Who's going to tell the parents?'

'You are. That's your punishment. You've put your toe in the water, and now you can ruddy well get right in and drown along with them.'

Robinson smiled wanly.

'One thing,' Fathers said. 'Why didn't you do something about the car?'

'I thought about that. But then I decided it wasn't

worth it. You could always run a computer check and my name'd stand out like a sore thumb.'

As the detectives left they paused in the small car-park in front of the Douglas and Jenks offices and looked at the silver-grey, four-door, B-registered BMW Fathers had seen earlier.

'How dumb,' said Cathy Gordon.

'What? To leave the car there? Or to stay mum when he came in this morning?'

'To get committed in the first place. To try to be mum.'

Fathers smiled. 'I suppose he felt he had no choice.'

'Too soft. Too kind.'

'That's why I'm not going to press it.'

Cathy Gordon looked at him. 'Softie yourself,' she said.

'Don't let on, especially not to Yarrow.'

'Not a kidnap at all,' she said. 'More its opposite really, when you think what he's the victim of. Poor boy.'

'Enough philosophising. Enough bleeding hearts. Back to crime.'

'That's what we've just been dealing with, or hadn't you noticed?'

'I said, enough philosophising.'

Has Anybody Here Seen Me?

Julian Symons

Out of the Underground train, along the platform, up the stairs, on to the escalator. Advertisements moving past, best pizza in London, it's mouthwateringly m-m-m-moreish, Michael Frayn play at Savoy, see-thru nightie that turns him on, Smirnoff the vodka, Morland's Can Find That Job You're Looking For, Dance all Night at the Fandango, Alligator Jeans Go Snap.

To the top, present ticket, up more stairs, out. Where? Why, he thought, looking at the bookshop on one corner, Great Newport Street beside it, news-stand nearby, the theatre showing *He Did What She Wanted*, a new comedy, I know this place, of course I do. Then, seeing the Underground entrance saying 'Leicester Square', he shook with laughter. All I had to do was look at the station name as I came out, silly me. Leicester Square station, just round the corner the Hippodrome, then the Square itself. *Used* to be the Hippodrome, now Talk of the Town, something like that. I know where I am, of course I do. Couldn't recognise Leicester Square, did you ever? No I never, no I never did.

So here I am but the question remains, most unfortunately the question remains. Not where, but who? Face up to it, the name's gone. Who knows it, who's seen me, am I the invisible man? Familiar lines came into his head, he had to restrain himself from singing them:

> Has anybody here seen me?
> M-e-double-e, me,
> Where can me be?
> I left home at half-past ten,
> Haven't seen myself since then,
> Has anybody here seen me-e-double-e,
>   me-e-double-e, me?

A clever little song, but its entrance into memory was disturbing. Something wrong with it, something he didn't want to remember, something that made movement imperative. He said aloud, 'No use standing here,' bought an evening paper, crossed the road, walking in a businesslike manner as if he knew where he was going. He passed a shop that showed in the window brass doorknobs, door knockers, bathroom fittings, gilded mirrors. Stopped to consider his reflection in a mirror.

A tallish man, thin, dark-blue jacket and trousers, mouse-coloured hair receding a little, smooth nearly delicate features, good figure, almost elegant really. Lines about the eyes though and, oh dear, as he looked more closely, some wrinkles in the delicate features. Age? Oh, say thirty-five – well, perhaps forty, no more than forty. Why should thought of age make alarm bells ring in his head?

And now that I've seen him: who is this stranger?

But *of course*, he mentally told the figure in the glass, there's really no problem in this case of lost identity. Just – it's so simple – just look at his wallet, credit cards, any stray envelopes bearing name and address that may be about his person. The figure in the glass felt its inner breast pocket. Nothing there. He watched with detachment as the figure, now a little agitated, felt in jacket, trouser hip pockets, dredging up some five pounds in coins, and a shopping list made on a piece of paper evidently torn from a memo pad. Fillet steak, new potatoes, courgettes. Is that my writing? The figure in the glass put the paper against the shop window to write on it, then checked himself. No pen.

Never mind, he told himself, no cause for alarm, I'm not lost, I know just where I am, could find my way without trouble around Central London, no trouble at all, I assure you. All that's happened is a temporary blackout, happens to almost everybody at some time or another. A blockage, like that caused by wax in the ear. In ten minutes or perhaps less something in my head will go *click* as the ear goes *pop*, and I shall remember.

A drink might help.

Within a hundred yards a pub revealed itself. The sign outside showed two men staring at each other, one a respectable whiskered top-hatted Victorian, the other a jaunty crouching creature, half-man and half-ape, arms stretching well below his knees. The pub was called The Jekyll and Hyde. He pushed open the Saloon Bar door, went in.

'What'll it be?'

'A pint of best bitter.'

Did he know this pub, did he often drink bitter? The place was crowded, but he saw a vacant seat at one table, sat down, drank some bitter, gave an involuntary shudder.

The other man at the table was thickset, sandy, with a sharp enquiring nose. 'Great weather we're having. Can't have enough of it far as I'm concerned.' The words were said challengingly, in apparent fear of contradiction.

He realised that he was hot, uncomfortably so, shirt clinging to him. He nodded.

'The wife now, she don't like it. Get out in the garden, I say, enjoy the sun while you can, don't get much of it, this ain't California. Know what she says? Too much sun gives you skin cancer. I ask you, how many days do we get like this in a year, ten, twenty? Say thirty, the most I'll give you is thirty.' The glare seemed to call for a response, but he did not make it. 'All right, thirty. And that gives you skin cancer, I say to her, thirty days in the sun, is that what you're telling me? No good though, she covers herself up like she was wearing one of those Arab things.'

'Yashmaks.'

'Right you are.' The man looked at him with respect. 'You a regular? Seen you in here before, have I?'

'If you'll excuse me, there's something I want to read in the paper.' It was true, he had an overwhelming feeling that the evening paper contained vital information about his identity.

'Suit yourself.' The man picked up his empty glass, ordered a refill at the bar, took it to another table.

He opened the paper, an early edition. He could not have said what he expected to find, perhaps a name he would recognise, perhaps a picture of the man in the shop mirror. He turned the pages quickly, not reading but looking for a name, a picture, something he felt must be there.

Nothing. Now he went through the pages more slowly, lingering over the news stories. On the front page discussions about an atomic pact, and in a separate panel 'This Time the Wolf Kills'. The Wolf, it seemed, was a burglar and rapist who had terrorised an area in South London. He was uncannily skilful in entering houses through skylights, windows closed but not locked, basement areas. He cased houses carefully, making sure that only one person was there, and that a woman. Mostly they were married, and the Wolf struck in the late morning or early afternoon. He threatened the woman with a knife, raped her, then took any jewellery he could find. In this case the woman had resisted, there had been a struggle, the Wolf had stabbed her to death. Significant clues, the story said, were being followed up by police.

What else? Scandal in a Home for Young Delinquents, Big Drugs Haul at Heathrow, Pop Star Tells All, Arson Suspected in City Fire, Man in Spy Enquiry Vanishes. 'Civil Servant James Hetherington, recently interrogated in relation to the missing Ministry of Defence papers, left his home in Clapham yesterday morning, and has apparently disappeared. His wife Jennifer said he left just as usual after breakfast, taking his briefcase and saying he might be a little late that evening . . .'

'Is this seat taken?'

A woman stood beside his table, glass in hand, half-smiling. He said it was free, and she sat down. A young woman, thirty-five perhaps, unobtrusively dressed, gold ring on wedding finger. Was there something about her he recognised? Now she did laugh, raised her glass. 'Seen enough?'

'I beg your pardon. It's just that I thought . . .'

'Yes?'

'Do we know each other?'

She looked at him over the rim of the glass, a short drink, probably gin and something. 'Well. What do you think?'

'I think perhaps we've met before.'

'Tell me the old old story. I mean, I wouldn't call that a new approach, would you?' Her voice was artificially refined.

'It isn't an approach. It's simply that I can't remember . . .'

'Where it was we met? That one's as old as the hills too. Never mind, I'm Rosemary. What's your name?'

'John.'

She had noticed the pause before he said it. 'That's not very original either. Are you going to buy me one, John? Gin and french.'

As he went up to the bar and ordered the drink he wondered: Do we really know each other or not? Can I tell her the truth? The barman seemed to look at him oddly. Perhaps they knew each other too, he was expecting to be greeted.

'Do we know each other?'

The barman had a toothbrush moustache, hair cut very short. 'How's that?'

'I've been in this pub before, thought I recognised you.'

'You looking for trouble?'

'Of course not. Why should you think so?'

'You stay your side of the counter, I'll stay mine, right?' The barman stuck his face forward, pores were visible in his broad cheeks. 'Or put it this way, I don't know you, you don't know me, let's keep it that way, right?'

Rosemary was reading his paper. 'I hope you don't mind.'

'Of course not.'

'You've spilt something, John, stepped in it too, from the look of it. Cheers.' He looked down and saw two dark patches on his left trouser leg, one near the bottom, the other above the knee. Another patch, or stain, marked his left shoe.

180

'This Wolf, I don't know what things are coming to, you're not safe in your own home. What you been up to then, John?'

Confession seemed inevitable. 'I don't know.'

'How do you mean, don't know?'

'This is important.' He leaned across the table, grasped for her hand, but she withdrew it. 'Do we know each other or not?'

She looked away. 'That's a funny question. It was you said we knew each other.'

'Please listen. I said my name was John, but I don't know if it is or not, I don't know what it is, I've lost my memory. I think I only lost it a little while ago.' He was conscious that the words must sound absurd, as he saw her looking from side to side as if in fear of attack. The overlay of refinement had gone from her voice when she spoke again.

'I'll tell you what I think, John, you're a bloody nutter. I'm a working girl, I thought you meant business, it wasn't me who started this what's your name lark. I don't know what you're after, but whatever the game is, I'm not playing. I'm going out of that door now and if you come after me I swear I'll turn you in. Now you remember that, *John*.'

She left the pub, hips swaying. As the door closed after her the barman stopped polishing a glass, stared at him as it seemed accusingly. He shook his head as if the action might help to shake those lost bits of memory back into place. Instead, it brought to the surface another line or two of that song:

> I'm an actress on the stage
> And I should be all the rage
> But I'm always losing *some*thing.

How did it go on? Da da *da*, da da *da*, then the last line of the verse, 'And now I've lost meself.' Very careless, John or whatever your name is, you'd better find yourself again.

He looked at the pub clock. Two-fifteen. As good a time as any other for discovering your identity. He folded the paper carefully, put it on the table, got up, left the pub.

A fine afternoon in London. Two-fifteen, by now two-sixteen. *I left home at half-past ten, Haven't seen myself since then*. Did I buy the fillet steak, if so, where is it? Let's hope I didn't leave it out so that the cat could get at it. Do you own a cat then, John? Don't know.

Take the first right, second left, leads down to the river. Is that so, how do I know it? But I do. Down to the river, on to the bridge, vault the parapet, no problem, it's quite low, then down down, an endless descent that lasts only seconds. The water, cold, dirty. Make no resistance. Finish.

That's what you may *think*, John, but things aren't that simple. Always a dozen busybodies around just waiting for people to jump off bridges, raise the alarm, strip off, jump in, life-savers to a man or woman. Man or woman created He them. But did He, is that so?

For that matter, they say the moment you hit the water you struggle, don't want it, never meant things to end like this, swim with a nice easy crawl to safety. Never meant to enter that cold river, officer, just leaning over the parapet to look at my reflection, Narcissus complex you might say, leaned that tiny bit too far.

Stop it, stop it, he said to himself – or had the words been spoken aloud? He took the first right. A narrow street this, small shops, shabby, seems familiar. News-agent's, antique shop Victoria Regina, 'we sell all the rubbish Grandma threw out', barber's pole, heads bent over basins, attendant waves and smiles. At me? Go in, ask, Excuse me, who am I? Have you seen me? Has anybody here seen me? Drawn a blank, Oh dear, thank you kindly, sorry you've been troubled. But where can me be?

A couple of lines of patter: *I'm so forgetful, you know, last night I got home, took me clothes off and tucked 'em up in bed, then hung meself up in the wardrobe.* But let's be frank about it, this is no joke. *Has* anybody here seen me? Waiting, waiting for the click of recognition.

It did not come. He took the second left, and at once felt uneasily: I know this. On the left there will be an Italian restaurant named Ruggieri, a cut-price men's clothing shop, a block of flats named Atlas Court. And on the right? The right was boarded up. There were cracks in the posters and he crossed the road, looked through. A half-demolished building stood there, a sign in front of it: 'For All Demolition Work Come To D. E. Stroyer.' On the damaged façade of the building the word 'Theatre' remained, and on the walls below two or three torn placards. One showed the picture of a top-hatted monocled Victorian toff, and said 'Burlington Bertie is One of the Boys', another was of a woman wearing an enormous picture hat, with 'Outrageous Olivia, Outré With Oomph' beneath.

'Good afternoon to you.'

He turned. A tramp perhaps, but if so a burly and upright one. Clothes old and shabby, trousers with old-fashioned turn-ups and slightly frayed at the bottom, but grey hair neatly brushed, and a waxed grey moustache giving an air somewhat military yet hardly genuine. The voice too had something assumed about it, rather as though it were being issued from a ventriloquist.

'Lookin' at the old place, then? Victim of the property

developers, a damned shame. And what do they do with it? Two years now, and it still isn't even properly knocked down. Just sittin' on it, every month it's worth another few thou. A demned shame I say.'

'Perhaps you can remind me, what was it called?'

The man stared. 'Remind you? Ay should say so. Remind you of the Old Tyme Theatre, that's extremely droll.'

He gestured at what lay behind the boarding. 'I've forgotten exactly your connection, I'm afraid.'

The man pulled at his moustache, faintly clicked his heels. His voice took on momentarily the stentorian tones of a circus barker. 'Percy Cudmore at your service, formerly sar'n't major in Her Majesty's Indian Army, now employed to keep this rabble in order. Remember now, old man? Kind of combined commissionaire and chucker-out. Not that there was any need for the chuckin' out line, though some of the lads got a bit above themselves at times. *You* remember that, or should do.' His left eye closed in an unmistakable wink.

'I'm afraid not.'

'If you say so. No offence meant, none taken, I hope.' He stood a little closer, garlic and beer discernible. 'Times are diff' for an ex-sar'n't major, old man. Can't even get a job as a pub bouncer, say I'm too old and not up to it, can you believe it? The same not true of your good self, I hope, you're lookin' remarkably well an' flourishin'. Wish I could say similar. If you happen to have a bit of foldin' money superfluous to present needs it'd be much appreciated.'

Here was somebody who knew him. What could be simpler than to say: I remember we were both associated with this theatre, but exactly what did I do there, who was I? But the words were literally unspeakable. He had a feeling of dread, his limbs trembled, his throat seemed choked so that he could hardly breathe. He opened his jacket, felt for the wallet that was not there, then buttoned it again hurriedly, aghast at what the opened jacket had shown. But Percy Cudmore seemed to have noticed nothing.

He felt in his pocket, found two of the golden coins, put them in the hand that almost surreptitiously received them, then took a step backwards to remove himself from the body so close to his own. Hand closed on coins, transferred them swiftly to pocket, encounter over. Hand sketched a near-salute, jeering rather than respectful, and the words too seemed jeering, though they were harmless enough.

'Left the old foldin' money at home, worried about gettin' mugged I dare say, very wise. Many thanks, old man. Do the same for you one day, I hope.' Now Percy Cudmore, done with him, walked up the road, fifty yards away turned into a pub.

Hand shaking, he unbuttoned the jacket again. The right side of his shirt was spotted and smeared with red, there were stains on the jacket lining. He buttoned it once more.

Now his actions became decisive. He walked down to the end of the road, crossed it. The river was there, as he had known it would be. He walked along beside it until he came to the bridge, but hardly glanced at the water. Left at the bridge, over the Thames. Now on the south side, he went through a minor maze of narrow streets without troubling to look at their names, steps unerring.

All this was a kind of sleepwalking. He had no idea of who he was, or what would be at the end of this apparently purposeful left-right, left-right. He no longer sought to find a name for himself. I am me, he thought, no need to look further. Has anybody here seen me?

Never mind whether they have or not, whether I left home at half-past ten or not. If I did hang myself up in a wardrobe and put my clothes to bed, it's nobody's business but mine. The only person concerned is m-e-e-double-e, me-double-e, me.

Steady now, only a song. Don't take it seriously. Petrol station on corner. Turn right.

But, honestly, admit it. I'm always losing something, and now I've lost meself.

Do I wish to find me, him or it?

He turned another corner, stopped still. This was a mews, the street cobbled, garages on either side, little houses above them. The houses had been tarted up, newly painted blue, pink, white. Pot plants outside the front doors. At the far end a knot of people, two or three police cars. He made his way towards them over the cobbles, treading delicately as a cat. Faces turned towards him expectantly. He smiled, nodded. Yes, I know you. It is me, not you, that has disappeared.

A copper in uniform at the door looked enquiring, but feet clattered on the stairs, a man appeared. 'Chief Inspector Hawkins, just the man we're looking for, come on up.' He followed the Chief Inspector up the stairs into the living room, then put hand to mouth in dismay.

It was, or had been, a pretty room. The Italian china ornaments on walls and tables in the shapes of gloves, shoes, opened books, were a little chichi, the *trompe l'oeuil* window opening on a country scene with real curtains over it was rather preposterous, the tubular chairs and tables were out of key with the ornaments and the window, but still it had been a pretty room. Now most of the ornaments were smashed, the curtain had been pulled down, lighting fittings were broken. Glass and china littered the floor.

'Somebody went a bit berserk, wouldn't you say?' Hawkins was rosy faced, smiling, his manner jolly. 'But you ain't seen nothing yet.' He led the way along past a tidy kitchen to a bedroom. There was blood everywhere here. It had spurted over the walls, marked the white carpet, there were splotches of it on the pink sheets. He shook his head, he could not have said why.

'Looking for the body? Went half an hour ago, no need to worry. Now then, sir. Your name is Oliver Raynes, and you share this delightful residence with one Archibald Burton, now the late Archibald Burton, agreed? And the said Archie had recently been showing an undue interest in a young actor by the name of Leon Padici, agreed? And according to your next-door neighbour, Archie had been communicating to you the idea that he'd prefer your room to your company as the old saying goes, he'd like you to move out and Leon to move in.

'And this same neighbour heard a most tremendous barney going on early this morning – couldn't help hearing, he says, the shouts and shrieks woke him up – as a conclusion to which Archie succumbed to attacks with a meat chopper from the kitchen, the assailant being apparently under the impression that Archie was a side of beef that needed carving. He then did the demolition job you've seen in the next room and exited into the street where the ever-watchful neighbour saw him. Or you.'

The words made no impact on him. He was staring at a poster on the wall which had escaped the general carnage, except for a spot or two of blood. It was one he had seen outside the theatre, showing the woman in the picture hat. It was signed: 'Dearest Archie, with all my love, Olivia.' The chief inspector was still talking.

'Now here you are, come back to save us the trouble of looking for you, which I must say is very helpful. And with marks that show just what a naughty boy you've been.' He wagged his round rosy head in reproof. 'I couldn't be sorrier, I'm one of your admirers.'

'Not me,' he said. 'It was not me. I could never have done such a thing. This is not me.' He took off his jacket, threw it on the ground, unzipped his trousers. 'Please. These are not mine. The clothes I wear are not me, nothing of all this is me. I am not me. Has anybody here seen me?' He looked wildly round, but the chief inspector was his only audience. His trousers dropped to the floor. Beneath them he wore frilly pants, lettered, 'Naughty But Nice.'

Hawkins laughed heartily. 'Your famous song, of course, *I left home at half-past ten, Haven't seen meself since then*. And very well you always delivered it. Pity the Old Tyme packed up. I used to enjoy those shows, took my old lady, we sang the choruses. Quite fancied you myself, as a matter of fact.' He laughed again, to show that this was a joke. 'And "I am not me," that sounds a promising line. It wasn't me hacked my friend to death, it was somebody else, please, judge, I wasn't there. Yes, very comical, I like it.' He restrained his amusement, as it seemed, with difficulty. 'But now, Oliver Raynes, I must ask you to put these clothes on again. I am arresting you on the charge of murdering Archibald Burton, and must warn you that anything you say may be used in evidence. So come along, Oliver. Or should I say Olivia?'